E

“Another great book by Cynthia Schroeder. I could not put it down. The story kept me wanting to know more about what happened with each turn of the page. It gave me smiles and tears. Well written!”

-Steven Kreps

“Cynthia Schroeder did it again! Once I started, it was really hard to put it down. I really liked her idea of the three different lives. Cynthia has a way of describing the characters and events that make you forget about the time. If everybody could see life in a different perspective, like Cassie did, there'd be a lot more happy people out there. This book really makes you look at what's really important in life. I really hope you keep writing. *Raggedy Ann and the Lost Girl*, *Raindrop* and now *They Call Me Missy*. I'll be waiting for the next one! You're 3 for 3!”

-Dean Linstad

“*They Call Me Missy* is a book that once you begin reading it, you will want to read it to the end to find out what is happening next. Her character reminds us that our lives can change without warning and that change can open us up to new beginnings.”

-Janet Engebretson

“Thank you Cynthia for another interesting and provocative book. It was indeed a pleasure to read it and observe your maturity and mastery as a writer. Keep up the good work.”

-Dennis Maasjo, Ed.D.

ALSO BY CYNTHIA SCHROEDER

Raggedy Ann and the Lost Girl

Raggedy Ann and the Lost Girl is an engaging and endearing story of how two completely opposite women come together and share a life experience they will never forget. Karen is a middle aged house wife who was fed up with her 3 children and inattentive husband. After a frustrating morning, she decided she had enough and ran from her life with no destination and no plans. While away, Karen meets up with Jessica, a homeless young lady who was taken away from her mother and placed in foster care when she was 8 years old. Karen and Jessica drive across the country in hopes to locate and reunite Jessica with her mother. Together, they share various memorable experiences during their journey which bond these two forlorn strangers to form a friendship that will be never forgotten.

Raindrop

Bobbie Thompson woke up to an annoying and constant beeping sound of a heart monitor. A physician was standing over her telling her that she was struck by lightning while out jogging that evening.

Although her physical wounds were healing, she soon realized the massive jolt of lightning left her with a case of heightened senses or ESP. She was able to hear, smell and see things that others could not. Suddenly, a young girl from long ago came to Bobbie in a vision bothering her days and nights which left her restless and unsettled. Bobbie knew she couldn't move forward with her healing process, or her life, until she resolved the secret of young girl's mysterious disappearance.

This is a memorable and enduring novel of heartache and forgiveness with surprising twists and turns that keep you enthralled until the end.

They Call Me MISSY

Joanne
Enjoy the read!
Cynthia Schroeder

CYNTHIA SCHROEDER

Wasteland Press
www.wastelandpress.net
Shelbyville, KY USA

They Call Me Missy
by Cynthia Schroeder

First Printing – July 2016
ISBN: 978-1-68111-123-0

Printed in the U.S.A.

0 1 2 3 4 5

Life One

CHAPTER ONE

I sat at my desk, looking at a blank computer screen shaking with anger. I could feel the tips of my ears heat up as the anxiety and irritation boiled inside of me. My frustrations were at their max and I was saturated to my core with incompetent people whom I was forced to work with. All I could do was to sit at my desk without any further annoyances or distractions, close my eyes and meditate allowing my internal anger to slowly subside.

Some people hit pillows, some cry, some scream, while others withdraw. The antidote I use for recovery from stress is to close my eyes and meditate. I have learned that meditation calms my nerves and allows me to have power and domination over my own emotions. I never allow vulnerability and weakness to control of my emotions at work or as far as that goes, at any place. I cannot recall the last time I have ever cried. Not even at either of my parent's funeral. I just took care of business, as that is what I do.

I just returned from a meeting where not one person on the committee did their homework or brought information back to the table. The meeting was a waste of an afternoon. Everyone was too busy, someone was on vacation; somebody else had to cover for another sick employee…blah, blah, blah and then it just happened…the one time in my career, I finally lost control in front of everyone. Since no one brought the information back to me, I couldn't move forward with the project that I have been working on for over a month. Their incompetence made me look bad to my customers and now I would not be able fulfill the contract that I had with them in the time frame agreed upon.

I leaned back in my chair even more; I just don't understand why people don't take their work and careers as seriously as I do. Trying to meditate my anger away, I was interrupted with laughing and loud noises coming from outside of my office. Still irritated, I got up and slammed my office door shut. I must have slammed it a little too hard because as the door slammed shut, a picture fell off the edge of my desk.

I bent down and picked up the picture realizing it was the most precious photograph I own. It was the photograph of my mother and me sitting on her bed together before she died. I was eleven years old and remember taking that picture as if it were yesterday. She was hugging me so hard that it hurt but even as a young girl I didn't complain as I knew my Mom was dying of breast cancer, so I sat there and smiled. She died quietly in her sleep several weeks after that picture was taken.

I was the only girl in the family and growing up with three older brothers made me tough. I had to keep up or get trampled on. After Mom died, Dad made it my chore and obligation to do all the cooking and baking for him and my brothers. That was a big responsibility for an eleven year old girl. Having three older brothers and a hard working father, I had to make many large meals and a lot of baked goods. The first few weeks, I think we lived on grilled cheese and hot dogs but I soon learned to venture out to other types of meals and fortunately, we all survived. I often think of growing up and fighting my way amongst three brothers, as well as the responsibilities that my dad placed upon me. That environment most likely molded and shaped me into the successful career person I am today.

I put the picture back to its usual resting place next to a photograph of my dad, myself and my three older brothers. Jordan and Joseph were the oldest and identical twins; they were fourteen years old at the time of the photo. Standing next to them was J.D. who was twelve years old. J.D. had the same name as my dad, Jerry Dean, who was named after Jerry Lewis and Dean Martin. To avoid confusion, everyone just called my brother J.D. instead of Jerry or Jerry Jr. I was the youngest and was standing in front of them all wearing the most hideous and ugly blue dress than anyone could have seen for that time era. That picture was taken the day of Mom's funeral. All of us had forced smiles on our faces. I believe that was the last picture we have together as a family.

Being only a year apart in age, J.D. and I were best of friends growing up. Through thick and thin we could always count on each other, whatever problem arose. We had to depend on each other for comfort, love, support, and just about everything else. Since Jordan and Joseph were twins, they were joined at the hip and did everything together leaving J.D. and myself out of their doings. Mom was gone and Dad had to work a lot of long hours to support us and pay for all Mom's medical bills which left J.D. and me to rely on and be there for each other. That was how life was until we all grew up and went our separate ways.

Dad died five years ago of an early and sudden heart attack shortly after Joseph's wedding. Not surprisingly after Dad's death, we all have drifted apart and have not been very good at keeping in touch with each other over the years. Since then, I have been hard at work advancing my career. Jordan is divorced with no kids and stationed in Hawaii at the military base and has no plans on ever leaving Hawaii or the military. Joseph is married with three kids and is an attorney. He has a busy life schedule working at his wonderful law office and taking care of his 'Barbie Doll' wife and their three perfect children. On the other spectrum there is J.D., my buddy and pal; he turned into an alcoholic and is currently roaming the country somewhere...usually in and out of treatment centers or shacking up with some desperate woman willing to take him in. The last time I heard from him, he called to tell me that he was in treatment in Florida near Joseph and informed me that he was devoted to kicking his addictions. Knowing I heard that a million times before I told him I loved him and that I wished him well with his continued efforts of sobriety.

Suddenly my phone rang interrupting my thoughts and bringing me back to the present time. It was my boss, the Vice President of the Company.

"Cassie, can you come to my office in a few minutes?" she asked.

I knew I was going to get disciplined or possibly fired for my behavior at the round table meeting that I just came from. I knew I stepped over the line at the meeting. Letting out a big sigh, I went to the bathroom to regain my composure before going to her office. I splashed some water on my face and fixed my makeup before meeting with her. I looked at myself in the mirror and liked what was staring back at me; a confident and a well put together female. I not only had the college degree but I had had the right look. I worked hard at keeping my body fit and my appearance desirable. I wore top of the line business and fashion clothing and my closet at home supported that as it was bursting at the seams with name brand clothes such as Michael Kors, Louis Vuitton, and Coach, to name a few.

I learned very early how to work the political aspect of corporate business and could smooze the pants off a preacher man if I wanted to but to top it all off, I had the drive and organizational skills to fulfill the total package. The combination of all of those assets made me quite a successful career woman. I have dedicated a lot of hard work and time to be successful as an individual while also bringing huge success for this company. I have every intention of continuing to climb the corporate ladder, whatever it takes.

My workaholic lifestyle and my career was everything to me and because of that, I missed most of my friends' and relatives' weddings and managed to lose two boyfriends in the past few years. Surely, my boss wouldn't fire me over one mishap within the ten years that I have been working here. I took a big breath in and out and left for her office.

The name plate next to her door said: Lois Bixby, Vice President. Her door was cracked open but I still knocked before she told me to enter.

"Hi Cassie, have a chair."

I sat down in the chair across from her desk and silently waited for the potential consequences that I was about to endure but yet ready to defend myself for the assets that I had brought to this company over the past years of my employment.

She broke the uncomfortable silence and started to speak as she remained looking down at the paper work in front of her. "Cassie, I was looking over your work history and noticed in the ten years that you have been here, you took off three days when your dad died. I personally recall sometime last year, making you go home on a Friday afternoon when I heard you were throwing up in the bathroom from the stomach flu. That was a total of three and a half days of time you have taken off since you were hired. You now have four entire months of accumulated vacation and sick pay that you have not used up or turned back in for reimbursement."

I nodded my head in agreement; acknowledging the amount she quoted seemed fairly correct and accurate.

"Cassie," she finally looked up from her papers and directly at me, "you are one of our very best employees and a great asset to our team here. I do not want to lose you but it seems you are wound up tighter than a drum. Your actions at the meeting today were so unlike you and just not acceptable. It doesn't reflect well on you, me as your director, or this company as a whole."

"I know I behaved inappropriately but with that said, their constant lack of obligations to our ongoing requests just happened one too many times. Someone had to point out their unaccountability and the domino effect that happens when they won't provide the needed information," I pleaded hoping that she would take my side of the situation.

"Cassie, things happen sometimes. Life happens, and not everything goes structurally as planned. When we set tight expectations for ourselves and others, it most often is so tight that it becomes too impossible to abide by. We have to account for occasional bumps in the road and with that frustrations are sometimes bound to happen, in any situation. Did you know that Margaret was covering for her employee who ended up in the hospital with bilateral pneumonia? That employee's back up was already on a planned vacation in Hawaii. Margaret had to do the job of three people at the same time, only to come to this meeting to be belittled and yelled in front of others."

She paused for a moment looking down at her papers on her desk again before looking back up at me, "I believe you have work burnout and I am asking you to take at the minimum, three to four consecutive weeks off to get yourself back to the happy and well rounded person you used to be."

"Three weeks? I cannot take three weeks off, I have three big projects going on right now and can't leave right in the middle of them," I exclaimed.

"Three to four weeks," she stated emphasizing the four. "The 'D21' project is a high risk concern and we both have been involved in those work groups and meetings. I know you have the lead on that project but since I have a working knowledge of what is going on there, I will take that project over from this point on. The 'Unit Three' project is almost finished now and can be passed over to Carol to finish up all the loose ends there. The 'Landrey' investigation can be put on hold until you return, since that is not high on the priority list for this time."

Hurt and bothered by this mandatory leave of absence, I pleaded, "I don't know; is this really necessary? I don't want to take vacation time. I am fine."

She stared right into my eyes and said, "I don't like to give alternatives but in this case, the other option is for you to hand in your resignation. I can see you get increasingly more wound up every week and your actions at the meeting today, just confirmed it. If you keep going at this pace, you will be no good to us as a company or yourself. We…I want you here, but not like this Cassie. As your boss and as your friend, I am telling you that you need to take this time off."

My boss never spoke to me in this way before so I knew she was dead serious and slumped back into my chair. "Okay, fine," was all I could muster up as I let out a sigh of frustration.

"I want you to spend the rest of your day cleaning up your e-mails and going over the finishing details with Carol and me on the two projects."

Defeated, I got up from the chair across from her and started for the door when she spoke up again.

"Cassie?"

"Ya?"

"I hope you understand that this is for your own benefit. You will realize there is more to life out there than working 24/7 at this place or any other place as far as that is concerned. This company will not fall apart while you are gone."

I gave her a half smile and nodded to appease her. I learned how and when to pick my battles. This was one battle I knew I was not going to win so I just replied, "Sure, I guess so."

It was 7:00pm before I finally got home. I threw my purse on the table; went straight for the wine rack and proceeded to crack open a bottle of my favorite Merlot. Knowing I didn't have to go to work in the morning, I poured myself an extra large glass after running it through the wine aerator. I took my first swallow allowing myself to enjoy tannins of the alcohol dance on my taste buds. I meandered to the living room and sat down on my couch pondering over the events of the day and what I was going to do with myself for the next three to four weeks.

I soon was into my second glass of wine, when I decided that I may as well go through the many weeks of mail that had been piling up on my coffee table. Although I am anal-retentive at work, I tend to neglect the things at home such as cleaning and going through mail and paying my bills in a timely manner. I started to throw all the flyers and newspapers in one pile for trash. I was placing all my bills in a second pile when I came across a hand written card addressed to me. Curious, I examined the envelope as I did not recognize the handwriting. I noticed it was post marked two weeks ago from California. I quickly opened it and saw that it was an invitation to a reunion next weekend for my college Sorority, 'Sigma Theta Psi' in Sacramento, California. Inside were the usual things such as a website address to register and the agenda, contact names of committee members as well as a few links for various hotels.

I had no desire to go back to California to reminisce about my college years so I threw it in the trash pile with all the other junk mail and continued on with the mail separation.

It was 8:30pm when I found myself taking my last swallow of wine while at the same time was pushing the 'CONFIRM' button on my laptop; booking a flight and hotel for Sunday afternoon to Sacramento. It was most likely the wine…well, I am sure it was the wine that coerced me to get adventurous and book the flight. I will probably regret it in the morning but, for now a sorority reunion is something for me to do and pass some of my time while off of work. I certainly couldn't look at these four walls of my townhouse for the next three to four weeks as I would surely go insane.

CHAPTER TWO

I was starting to dose off when I heard the intercom go on. "To comply with airline regulations, please verify that all of your electronic devices, such as your cell phones and computers, are turned off for the rest of the flight. Thank you."

What an odd thing to announce when we were over two hours into the flight. I reached for my purse on the floor, pulled out my cell phone and confirmed it was completely shut off. I looked over at the fat man next to me who was snoring and obviously uninformed of the announcement. I could see a few others around me were checking their phones and I-Pads while the flight attendant walked down looking from side to side assuring that all electronic devices were turned off.

After the flight attendant walked up and down the aisle a few times, I watched her go into the cockpit and talk to the pilots. Assuming all was well, I closed my eyes again in hopes to get a little cat nap in before we landed. Just as I was staring to drift off for the second time, the loud speaker came back on again.

"This is captain Thorsgood. Not too alarm anyone, but our aircraft is having a small electronic malfunction. At this time it is not a serious issue; however, in order to assure the safety of the passengers and crew, we have made arrangements to make an unscheduled stop in Salt Lake City. Fortunately, there is another plane available to finish up the rest of your flight to Sacramento. Once we land, you can deplane. As you leave the gate, the gate attendant will hand out new boarding passes for your replacement flight. Extra gate attendants will also be available if you have complications with any connecting flights or questions that you may have. It will most likely take about forty-five minutes to "pull up" the replacement aircraft and transfer everyone's baggage. We at Star Airlines, apologize for any inconvenience this may have caused. Thank you."

A bunch of disgusted 'sighs' were let out by the passengers. For once, I was glad that this didn't affect any plans that I made as I had no other connecting flights or anyone to meet me at the Sacramento airport.

A few minutes later and just on the edge of darkness, I could see the lights of a large city to the far off distance. Again the intercom went on with the Captain's announcement, "Attendants, please prepare the flight for landing."

The flight attendants did their typical walk down the aisle with garbage bags, collecting trash and assuring that everyone was buckled in as well as trays being up and seats in their upward positions. A few minutes thereafter, the flight attendants took their seats facing the passengers. I could feel the pressure in my ears as we slowly descended. Although it wasn't too apparent, it seemed like the plane thrust upward again instead of landing. As we went upward, the plane started to turn right and began, what seemed to be, a large circle in the air. I looked around to see if anyone else noticed the dip and then re-ascent, however, everyone seemed unaware and unaffected to the change in pressure. I thought maybe the pilot may have overestimated his landing measurements and circled around again to make another attempt.

Looking at the lights below me, I watched as we circled around the lighted city again. Twenty minutes later and what seemed like a full circle, the plane started its descent. Again, just when I thought we were going to land, the plane ascended again to a higher altitude. This time I looked around and I could see a few people talking softly to each other and pointing out the windows. I looked up at the flight attendants who seemed to be unaffected by the twice attempted landing. Knowing the flight attendants have flown hundreds and thousands of flights before and were unaffected, I felt more confident that there was nothing to be concerned about.

We circled the sky again, but this time the plane seemed to take a larger circle than before, taking about 30 minutes or more to circle around the city. By this time, I knew people would be getting irritated and angry at missing any future connections they will have from all the delays.

Once around the city for the third time, the plane started its descent and again just when I thought we were going to land, the plane flew back up into the sky. This time, the passengers were starting to talk a little louder. My eyes gazed upon the lead flight attendant who was just hanging up the phone on the wall, just above her head. I watched her as she unbuckled herself to go into the cock pit and close the door behind her. About five minutes later, she came back out and sat back in between the other two attendants. I watched her as she cupped her hand over her mouth as she whispered into the other flight attendants ears telling them something unknown to the other passengers.

Shortly thereafter, the click of an intercom came on again. As soon as we heard the click of the intercom, you could have heard a pin drop in the airplane as everyone wanted to hear what was going on. "This is Captain Thorsgood again. I earlier announced our aircraft was having some electronic problems. The issue that we are currently having is that some of the electronic displays on our dashboard are not displaying or lighting up. With that said, we have been unable to determine if the landing gear has deployed. We have circled the control tower three times to see if they were able to physically visualize if our landing gear is down. However, due to the fact that some of our exterior lights are also not functioning from this electrical problem and it is no longer daylight outside, flight control are unable to ascertain if our landing gear has deployed or not."

Some people on the plane were making some whimpering noises as others were 'ssh'ing' them so that they could continue to hear what the else the captain was going to say.

"Presently, we are now low on fuel and have no other option than to land with the hopes that they are down. Rescue and emergency teams are on the runway for standby assistance for aid and rescue in lieu of any potential emergencies. Please refrain from using your cell phones or any other electrical devices at this time. Flight attendants, please prepare for emergency landing."

At this time everyone started to freak out. I could hear some women starting to cry out loud. I looked over across the aisle and saw an older couple kiss and hold each other's hands as they smiled at each other. The fat man next to me was perspiring heavily as beads of sweat ran off his forehead.

The flight attendant came on over the intercom. "Please try and remain calm. Make sure you safety belts are buckled and tightly secured. The oxygen masks should not come down since we are able to make a controlled descent; however, if they do deploy, make sure you place the mask on yourself first and then help any others that are in need of assistance. If this landing becomes uncontrolled, we have two emergency exits in the rear, two on each side and one in the front. The isles will be lit for clear exit. DO NOT rush. At this time, I need everyone to put their head down to your knees and wrap your arms around you legs until we land."

I did as she said and looked over at the fat guy next to me who could barely bend over. His eyes were closed and he was white as a ghost. I looked down and he was taking a photo of his family out of his wallet and then held it tightly in his hand. I should be thinking about my life, my family, etc. but all I could think of is that if we are going to die, my last vision was going to be of this old fat guy. Why couldn't I have had the opportunity to sit next to Brad Pitt or one of the Chippendales? At least my last vision on earth would be somewhat more pleasant than what I was stuck with next to me.

Then, the thought came to me that if we were going to crash, this fat guy could be a good cushion for me and help me stay alive. I also thought that if we land and I am still alive, I am not waiting for this guy to get out of my way. I was going to unbuckle my seat and jump over him faster than I have ever moved, regardless if he is dead or alive. With those thoughts, I wondered when I became so insensitive and bitter and was suddenly ashamed of my character and who I became to be.

This was it. My life as I knew it, was ending right here, right now on this plane. I had so much more to do, dreams to fill and goals to set that I had so carefully planned out for myself. I realized I didn't get accomplished everything I needed to do in life.

At that moment, I thought of my Dad and my Mom and how they are both dead now. I remember going to church and Sunday school as a very young girl before Mom died. After she died we never went again. I think Dad questioned his faith and had reservations of God Himself so we never went to Church again. To be perfectly honest, it made me doubt if there was a God in heaven as well. If there was a God, why did he take my Mom away from me when I needed her the most? My Mom had faith though. Her favorite verse in the Bible was Jeremiah 29:11. I remember that was her favorite because she insisted that I memorize it before she died: "For I know the plans I have for you, declares the Lord, plans to give you hope and a future." While she was laying there dying, did she foresee my future or maybe this moment in my life? Why else would she make me memorize it and not my brothers? Was she setting me up for this moment?

I now joined the others and for the first time in years, I silently started to sob to myself. Hoping there was a God, I quietly said a prayer for God to give me a hope and a future. I was not ready to die.

Although it was only minutes, it seemed like hours before we finally touched down. The plane bounced once from the tires as they hit the runway. When the tires first hit, the entire plane screamed with terror only to be followed by screams of relief and cries of joy. We landed without incident.

The plane slowly crept up to the tarmac until it came to a complete stop. Glad that I was towards the front, I grabbed my carry-on bag from the overhead storage and quickly moved off the plane. I grabbed my re-boarding pass from the lady at the desk and headed directly to the bar. I turned slightly and noticed a few others were not far behind me and going in the same direction. Still shaken from the ordeal which I just encountered, I found a spot at the closest bar and saw an open seat near the front entrance. I plopped down on the bar stool keeping my carry-on bag next to my feet.

"What can I get you?" asked the bartender.

"Two shots of Patron with salt and lime," I said without hesitation.

"You got it," as he turned away to get my drinks.

"A double Tequila? Must have been some flight," said a deep voice beside me.

I looked over to my right. I was so determined to get to the bar and order a drink; I didn't even notice the man that I sat next to. "You have no idea," I exclaimed.

Just then the bartender brought over my Tequilas and I shot each one down without hesitation. The bartender stood there, not walking away knowing that I was going to down them in seconds assuming I would need something else.

"Would you like anything else," he asked.

"I have time for another quick one." I stated.

Before I had a chance to order the man next to me said, "You should have the bar's 'Bahama Mama'. I am drinking one and it is really good and refreshing."

"Okay, I will," I replied.

"Make it two," the man told the bartender. "On me." The man then turned to me and introduced himself, "My name is John." He smiled at me and when he did, I took note that he was a fairly good looking man with a square jaw line and crystal ocean blue eyes. His blondish-brown hair was slicked back with little curls in the back but he had somewhat of a scared face from acne. His teeth were in poor hygiene as well, as if he didn't get good dental care as a child.

"I am Cassie, and thank you for the drink."

"So tell me why you needed the double Tequila."

Before I had a chance to respond, the bartender had already brought over two drinks with a pineapple slice in each one.

"Cheers," I said to John as we clicked glasses. I was so happy to be alive, I just wanted to celebrate.

After our toast, I went on to tell John about the electrical problems of the plane. I was in the middle of the story when out of nowhere my carry-on bag fell over next to me. Perplexed as to I why my carry-on bag would have fallen over, I bent down and put it back up on its wheels. I took another big swig of my Bahama Mama and then kept on telling him about my frightening airplane landing story.

It was a few minutes later when I started to feel dizzy and things started to blur. "Wow, I think that Tequila is starting to hit me or this Bahama Mama is loaded with booze," I stated as I fanned myself with my hand. My ears were starting to ring slightly. I looked over at John who was pulling money from his wallet to pay for the drinks.

"Maybe you should go to the ladies room and splash some water on your face," he stated as I saw him put his cash on the bar for our drinks.

By now, I was having a hard time even answering him. I nodded my head up and down persecuting myself for taking those two shots of Tequila back to back. I could see John talking to me again but it was like he was speaking to me in an echoed voice. I thought I heard him say, "Here let me take your bag and walk you to the rest room so that you can freshen up." He grabbed my upper arm and helped me off of my bar stool. Once out of the bar, I could feel his arm go around my waist as if we were a couple.

Life Two

CHAPTER THREE

I am freezing. Why am I so cold? I reached over to pull my blankets over me, only to find there weren't any. I opened my eyes and saw clouds within a blue sky above me. I realized I was not in my bed but somewhere outside. I could hear car traffic in the near distance and little farther off, the "beep, beep, beep" from a large work utility truck backing up. The stench of rotten meat and coffee grounds suddenly infested my nostrils, making me suddenly queasy.

I rolled over on my side and lifted my upper torso to rest on my left elbow. When I did, my head immediately throbbed with pain. I reached up with my left hand and flinched as I felt a soft and swollen spot on the left side of my head above my ear and behind my temple. I brought my hand back only to note that my fingers were free from any fresh blood but did notice, what appeared to be some flakes of dried blood in my hair.

I looked around my immediate surroundings and understood why it smelled like rotten meat. I was lying upward in piles of garbage bags which were stacked up next to a rusty and overflowing dumpster. I attempted to sit up fully and when I did, I felt more pain and pressure in my crotch and anal area. I tried to stand, thinking that if I took the pressure from my bottom, the pain in that area would dissipate. I grabbed onto the dumpster to help me get to my feet. Still feeling queasy and now a bit dizzy, I managed to stay standing but decided to rest my forehead on the corner of the dumpster to keep from falling. While resting my head and body on the corner of the dumpster I could see that I had one white sandal on my left foot but my right foot was bare. I performed a quick scan of my immediate surroundings but was unable see my other sandal anywhere in the immediate vicinity.

Taking a minute to gather my composure, I realized I was in a back alleyway behind an old brick building; most likely a business with apartments on the upper levels.

Still feeling queasy, dizzy and in pain, I started to walk toward the traffic on the nearby street. With every step I took, my head throbbed and my crotch wrenched with pain as if I just delivered a ten pound baby. I made it to the street where I was hit by the warm morning sun. I walked up to a nearby lamp post and I sucked up against it, allowing the heat from the warm metal to penetrate my body and warm my bones.

New smells suddenly filled my nostrils. I looked up the street and saw the familiar golden arches of McDonalds. My mouth was dry as my tongue stuck to the roof of my mouth as I opened and closed my mouth. I was thirsty and needed a drink of water; or a drink of anything for that matter and headed in the direction of the golden arches.

Wearing only my one sandal, I slowly staggered up the street toward the golden arches until reaching the parking lot. I had to stop and rest and leaned myself against the brick fence that surrounded the backside. A few minutes passed as I regained my breath and energy and ventured onward toward the front door.

Before entering the restaurant, I paused and saw the reflection in the glass staring back at me. It was someone I didn't recognize. It was a young lady in her late twenties or early thirties. The reflection stared back at me. I finally decided to lift my left hand and as I did, the reflection in the window mimicked my actions. The spaghetti strap on her top was torn. I looked down at my shirt and it also was torn and laying over my shoulder. I attempted to fix the strap and again the image in the glass reflected my actions. It was then that I realized I was looking at myself. I had dark brown hair. I was dirty and disheveled, but more so, I was foggy and confused as I didn't know who I was, where I am (other than at McDonalds) or why I am here.

In the reflection behind me, I saw a young family come up behind me who were laughing and holding hands. As they came closer to me they stopped laughing and became quiet. The little boy holding his mother's hand looked up at me with his somber eyes and fat little cheeks. Not saying a word, they bypassed me and walked in the door next to me. I decided to follow them inside so that I could use the rest room and clean up and get something to drink. I reached for my purse to see how much cash I had on me only to realize that I didn't have a purse. I looked around my skirt to see if I had any pockets where I may have some money; however, my skirt had no pockets. I scooted in behind the family anyway and walked to the bathroom.

Fortunately the bathroom was empty. The first thing I did was head for the sink and turned on the water. I cupped my hands under the faucet to gather water and quickly slurped it up alleviating the immediate dryness of my mouth. Next, I went to the nearest stall to relieve myself. When I sat down, the pressure of my bottom became painful once again and when I began to urinate, it burned as if my entire crotch was raw as hamburger. The sting was so painful that tears came to my eyes as I gasped for a breath. Instead of wiping, I dabbed that area to prevent any further pain. Before I threw the tissue into the toilet, I looked at it and saw small traces of blood on the tissue. I spread my legs and looked down and saw black and blue bruising on the inside of my thighs as well as on my outer labia. My inner labia were fiery red with some of the skin rubbed off. Without a mirror, I couldn't see back very far but I could feel with my fingers a couple of tears around my anus and vaginal opening. I knew I must have been violently raped but for some reason couldn't remember any of it.

When the stinging pain subsided, I got up from the toilet. I went to the sink and washed the dirt from my face only to see that same stranger looking back at me. Who am I and why can't I remember anything? After the grime was washed from my face, I studied the female reflected in the mirror before me. My skin was soft and ivory with a small bruise on my lower left jaw line. My eyes and hair were brown and I could see my eyebrows were waxed and groomed professionally. As I reached up to touch my face, I noticed I must have had a French manicure with acrylic nails on as I only had two nails left on my left thumb and left pinky finger.

While I was looking at myself in the mirror, a customer came in to use the other stall. While she was in the other stall, I took that opportunity to wash my hands and upper torso as best as I could. I then wet a couple of paper towels with hot water; took them back into the other open stall and dabbed the blood and sticky substances off of my private areas. I left the bathroom feeling a little better after I had washed and cleaned myself up a bit.

Knowing I didn't have any money for food or something to drink I started for the front door. I was almost there when I encountered a large woman, probably in her forties, speaking in a raised and stern voice towards an older and what appeared to be, a homeless bag lady. The large woman had a McDonalds work outfit on and a name tag that said: "Gladys Marquardt, Team Manager."

"Beverly, I told you not to come in here unless you are buying something. If you need food, you go to the Shelter or down to the Salvation Army." Looking my way she then said, "And that goes for you too, missy!"

I looked around and noticed everyone was now staring at me. I looked around again and realized she was speaking to me. She must think that I am a homeless person too and with the homeless bag lady.

The homeless bag lady grabbed my arm and said, "Come on Missy, we don't want this dog food anyway." She pulled me along through the front doors with her. Confused, I followed the homeless bag lady outside thinking it should be all right since this bag lady called me Missy as well. She must know me and my name is obviously "Missy".

I followed the homeless bag lady out of the building and across the back of the paved parking lot only to go toward, yet, another dumpster. She sat down on the curb and I carefully sat next to her flinching as the pressure of the hard surface pushed on my bottom.

The homeless bag lady started to laugh out loud for no apparent reason. Then she started a distorted conversation with herself that was incomprehensible to the normal person. I just stared at her in awe at the lack of her cognition and awareness of her surroundings. I almost started laughing but was too worn out to even question her actions. Not only was she talking like a crazy woman, she looked like a funny crazy person too! She had several long gray and course hairs growing from her chin. Her lips were puckered inward due to the lack of a full set of teeth and her graying and scraggly looking hair was pulled back into a pony tail. She wore brown, large framed glasses that seemed to be straight out of the 1980's. More so, she stunk as if she hadn't bathed or showered in weeks or maybe even months.

Suddenly, without pause from her crazy talk, she turned to me and said, "Are you hungry?"

"Yes, I am starved but I am more thirsty than hungry," I replied.

"If we wait a little longer, they'll throw out the morning breakfast food that has been under their heaters too long. They do that when they switch over to their lunch menu. It's usually a little dry, but it's warm and it something to put in your belly." Then she stood up and started to dig in the dumpster and pulled out a cup that was half full, of what I assumed was some soda. She took a sip and then handed the rest over to me to drink. Appalled at the thought of drinking someone else's flat warm soda that has been in the garbage for...who knows how long, I decided to drink it anyway. I had to drink something. I was still nauseated and my head was hurting really bad. I felt feverish and cold at the same time. I didn't know if it was from being raped, if I was just dehydrated, or both.

A few minutes later, as clockwork, a McDonald's employee brought out a black garbage bag and threw it in the dumpster. When the employee turned back towards the restaurant, the homeless bag lady pulled the bag back out of the dumpster and started to rummage through it. She pulled out some meat, eggs and biscuits; obviously parts of breakfast sandwiches that fell apart when thrown into the bag. She put some meat and eggs between some biscuits and gave me a couple of newly created breakfast sandwiches and then made a couple for herself.

As we began to eat, she said, "I am Beverly but you can call me Aunt Bev. Most everyone that knows me calls me Aunt Bev."

I smiled at her for her help and kindness and said, "Thank you Aunt Bev. I…I am Missy," I hesitantly replied.

We sat in silence for a few minutes eating our recreated meal and enjoying the shade from the hot sun when a black car pulled up beside us. The window rolled down and a woman's arm reached out with a bright bangle bracelet. She had a five dollar bill in her hand. Aunt Bev stood up and took it from the woman in the black car and sat back down beside me as the people in the black car drove off.

"Why did that person just give you money?" I asked.

"I suppose she thinks we need it," Aunt Bev replied.

By this time, I am more confused than ever. "Aunt Bev, have we met before and do I live around here? For some reason I am a bit fuzzy. I am not feeling very well at all and for some reason I don't remember anything."

"Not that I can recall but then I meet a lot of people and my memory is not as good as it used to be. Where do you usually stay?" she asked.

I had to stop and think before I finally answered, "I don't know. I don't know where I live."

"Well, when we are done eating here, you can come along with me and we'll find you a place to stay until you feel a little better. You can sleep there for a bit if it is okay with the others."

We finished up our food and started back down the street. As we walked, she went into the trance of talking to herself again making me wonder if I should follow this crazy lady or not. At this time, I didn't feel like I had any other options and being so sick, I certainly wasn't in any kind of shape to fend for myself. I had to take any act of kindness and any help I could get right now.

It was about ten minutes or so later when we arrived at an old abandoned building. I was thankful to finally get to our destination because I didn't think I could have walked another step in my condition. As it was, I had to stop and rest for a couple of minutes along the way preventing us from getting here any quicker. I was breaking out in cold sweats and my head was throbbing something awful. I felt as if I was going to black out at any moment. I just wanted to lie down as I knew I was fading fast. Aunt Bev led me around the back side of the building. Once there, she took a board off a window and led me inside placing the board back on the window.

"Make sure you always put that board back up so that people don't know we are down here," she said as she motioned for me to follow her. We walked down a dark staircase and into a room that was branched off to the side. In this room were four makeshift beds with some personal paraphernalia by each bed. One bedroom, if that is what you call it, had blankets hung on wires; separating it from the others.

"Did you's bring me some breakfast Aunt Bev?" A booming man's voice from behind made me jump as I let out a little yelp.

"Well, who do we's have here? I's so sorry, as I didn't mean to spook ya," said the man as he let out a chuckle.

"This is Missy from McDonalds and this is Bob the Magician," said Aunt Bev introducing us.

"Missy McDonalds? Well it's nice to meet you Missy McDonalds," as he reached his hand out to shake mine.

It was obvious that he didn't hear or understand Aunt Bev that she brought me from McDonalds. I decided not to clarify or explain the misunderstanding as I was too exhausted and drained to explain otherwise and just went with it.

"Hello, it's nice to meet you too. Do you live here as well?" I asked as I forced some more energy to shake his hand back.

"Yes em. I's live in this here bed," as he pointed to the bed that had the blanket separating it from the others.

I smiled and nodded as he seemed so proud of his area.

Aunt Bev spoke up, "Missy needs a place to stay and I thought maybe she could take Skinny's bed since he hasn't been around for a few weeks."

"I reckon that'd be alright but if Skinny comes back, you's gunna have to give him his spot back."

"Thank you and I will," I stated with appreciation. I was so exhausted and sore that all I wanted to do was to lie down and rest and right now and any place would do.

Skinny's bed was across from Bob the Magician's bed. It was essentially a stack of old blankets layered to look like a bed. Next to it was a cardboard box with a candle and some matches on top of the box. Inside of the box was another white closed container. Aunt Bev told me to keep away from Skinny's personal stuff that he had in his white container.

"You can use his candle for light as long as you replace the matches," said Aunt Bev. She pointed out one small window that wasn't covered with boards that caught the morning sun. "After the sun goes behind the building, the room gets fairly dark and then you have to use a candle or a flashlight to see anything."

"Who sleeps in the fourth bed?" I asked noting it was empty.

"That is Sunny's bed. She comes and goes. Never know when she will show up."

I didn't even ask who Sunny was. I just laid down on Skinny's dirty blankets not caring about anything else other than getting off my feet to relieve the downward pressure from my bottom and hopefully alleviate my horrible headache and weakness.

I don't know if it was hours, days or weeks that passed but I was awoken to a funny odor and sat up in my bed. I was confused for a few seconds wondering where I was at but soon remembered that I was in the abandoned building that Aunt Bev brought me to. Daylight was peeking through the lone window in the makeshift room of beds. I was drenched in sweat and the air around me was making me cold. I must have been feverish and out of it until now. I barely recall Aunt Bev feeding me a sandwich and sucking water from a straw out of a plastic cup filled with water.

I rubbed my eyes and stretched and realized that I had to pee really, really bad. I had to find a bathroom. With a quick look around, both Bob the Magician and Aunt Bev were not in plain sight but a very petite and tough looking female was in the bed next to me. She was in the process of lighting up a one-hitter of weed. I wondered if that was Sunny but didn't want to take the time for introductions since my bladder was about to burst. I got up and looked around for my shoes, only to remember that I only had one white sandal.

"Where is the bathroom?" I said to the woman smoking dope.

"Outside or wherever you can find one."

"Really?" I ask in surprise.

"This isn't the Hyatt Regency, ya know," she replied sarcastically.

Without responding and my one shoe on, I found my way to the steps which led outside. The sky was dark overhead as if a thunder storm was in foot. The air was hot and thick as if you could cut the humidity and smog with a knife giving no respite from the dark and unventilated area of the basement of which I just came from.

I found a secluded place behind a tree in which to relieve myself. It was disgusting and humiliating but I was thankful I had a long broom skirt on to hide what I was doing. I remembered the stinging pain when peeing at McDonalds but this time thankfully, the pain was much less.

When I was done peeing I went back and leaned against the building. I took in my surroundings trying to recall the events that brought me here to this abandoned building from the dumpster. It all was very strange and confusing. This lifestyle cannot be who I am or what I normally do and this didn't feel right or a typical routine for me. I decided to go back into the building to see if I could find Aunt Bev and maybe get some answers to some of the puzzling questions that engulfed my thoughts. In the mean time, I was in hopes that the woman smoking weed wouldn't be mean to me again.

I barely made it back to the bedroom area when I encountered Bob the Magician standing next to the mean lady. I stopped in my tracks not knowing if she was going to beat me up or tell me to leave or what exactly.

"So, where did you come from?" she asked rather appalled that I was in her 'private hideout'.

Before I had a chance to answer, Bob the Magician answered for me. "Dis here is miss Missy McDonalds. She's gunna stay in Skinny's bed till he's gets back."

"I know what her name is," she snapped at Bob the Magician. "Aunt Bev already told me. I asked her where she came from, but whatever," replied the mean lady. "Skinny most likely isn't coming back anyway. If he hasn't been here by now he's either dead or back in detox or treatment again."

The mean lady was rough looking and I was intimidated by her looks and her attitude. She was probably in her late thirties or early forties but her weathered appearances made her look fifty. Her hair was ratty and matted in some places as if she hadn't brushed it in days. Her skin was leathery and her eyes lids were puffy while darkness hallowed low half moons below her eye sockets.

"Well then dis here is Miss Sunny," said Bob the Magician proud of his introduction to Sunny.

"It's nice to meet you," I smiled as I carefully sat down on the Skinny's bed, trying not to strain my bottom.

Aunt Bev walked in about that time with a bag of cold pancakes. I assume she retrieved them from the McDonalds dumpster. She offered some to everyone and I decided to take one out of courtesy.

Realizing how hungry I was, I started to pick little pieces from the pancake and started to eat it while Aunt Bev went off on another one of her tantrums. This time, she was on her way outside waving her hands in the air, mumbling something about forgiveness and Jesus the Savior.

"Weez were wondering if you was ever gunna wake up," stated Bob the Magician.

"I wonder how long I slept," I stated more of a thought verses a direct question to either one of them.

"You were out like a light for a couple of days," replied Sunny.

"A couple of days? I was sleeping that long?"

"You sure were. We weren't sure if you were going to come around or not. You were pretty out of it. Aunt Bev brought you food and water a couple of times a day. She took good care of you."

"I barely remember eating and drinking only once. I think I was running a fever."

"You sure were. She patted down your forehead several times with a cold cloth. She even went out and bought a bag of ice with some of her change money. She put the ice all over you to try and cool down your body when you were burning up."

Bob the Magician must not have wanted any more conversation about that topic as he grabbed a small suitcase from beneath his bed and followed Aunt Bev back up the stairs only to leave me alone with Sunny. Suddenly, I felt very vulnerable being alone with Sunny. I didn't know what else to do other than just say something to break the silence.

"Why do they call him Bob the Magician?" I asked.

"Cuz he is a magician," said Sunny. "I guess he used to have a fairly good show in Las Vegas but according to Bob, his partner screwed him over and took all his ideas, contracts, and his money leaving Bob out in the cold. He moved to Reno trying to get a new start but didn't do so very well. I don't know how he ended up here. Bob doesn't even have a high school education and not the smartest guy on this earth so wasn't able to handle the management part of the trade. Now he just hustles magic on the street for a few dimes and nickels here and there. He says he has no family, so that is what he does. Sad story," she stated as she curled her lip down and shook her head back and forth. "But then, don't we all have a story to tell," she asked not really expecting an answer to her question.

"That is too bad," I stated.

"Why do they call Bev, Aunt Bev?" I asked emphasizing on the Aunt.

"I guess there was a girl living here for a while who said that Bev looked like her aunt so she always called her Aunt Bev. Shortly thereafter everyone just started calling her Aunt Bev and it just stuck after that. That was before I got here to Salt Lake City, so I have always known her as Aunt Bev. She is a good person, just crazy as a bat."

"We are in Salt Lake City?" I asked surprised.

This time Sunny looked at me as if I was the one who was crazy as a bat. "Yes, ma'am, there's no place like home."

I thought quietly for a while trying to think if I have always lived here or trying to remember anything of my home and again it was blank and decided to go back to asking her some more questions.

"What about Skinny? Why is he called Skinny?"

Sunny laughed, "Because he's so skinny! He doesn't have a fat cell on him."

"Does everyone have nick names here?"

"Pretty much," said Sunny

"So, is your name Sunny or is that a nickname as well?"

"I go by Sunny Delight, but my real name is Darla; Darla Brettendorf."

"Sunny Delight?" I repeated curiously. "That's a rather unique name. Why do you use Sunny Delight as your name instead of Darla?"

Sunny smiled. "First of all, Darla is boring for someone living on the street. I mean seriously, can you imagine someone saying, 'Let's go hang out with Rocky, Snake and Darla Brettendorf!' Shit man, I would get beat up for just having a name like that," as she shook her head back and forth giggling.

I laughed along with her as it did sound rather funny, especially the way she made fun of it and mocked her name and living situation. I was starting to like this person. She was more personable than my earlier encounter with her.

"One of my first days here, I was walking along the sidewalk in front of a strip mall," she continued on with her story. "A semi truck was delivering sodas and drinks to the convenience store across the street when I noticed the delivery truck driver didn't latch the back door of his truck before he took a load of sodas into the store. I was desperately thirsty and hungry, so while he was inside, I ran to the back of the truck and grabbed the nearest thing I could get my hands on and took off running. I didn't even know what I grabbed but it happened to be a case of Sunny Delight."

"It was a really hot day and when I brought it back here to the Condo, I shared them with everyone. They really appreciated it. Back then we had, believe it or not, nine people sleeping here. Since I was new here and they really didn't know my name, they just started calling me 'the Sunny Delight girl'. Thereafter, it just was Sunny Delight. I use that as my street name now."

"Well, I guess there are worse names," I smiled as I shrugged my shoulders.

"Yes, I would guess there are....like DARLA!" she responded in jest.

"You called this the Condo, was it a condominium at one time?" I asked out of curiosity.

"No, I think it was an old business building long ago, but I am not sure. As far as the name of Condo...it is where everyone sleeps and hangs out so we just call it the Condo. Now, girlfriend, I have to catch up on some sleep." With that, she rolled over and almost immediately started a light snore...even though it was mid morning.

With Sunny fast asleep and Bob the Magician and Aunt Bev gone, suddenly I was left alone to tend to myself. I decided to explore the building that we were in; outside of this room known as the Condo. I grabbed the candle and matches in case there were no windows to light up my view. I knew the stairs were to the left, so I turned right to go down the hallway. As expected, it was dark and I lit my candle. After a few steps, I decided it was rather creepy and not sure I wanted to go any further. The candle didn't give off a whole lot of light. I had to raise the candle high to see what was in front of me and then down again by my feet to assure my footage was clear to walk.

The walls around me had various graffiti signs painted on them but I noticed both the walls and graffiti paintings were dusty as if no one had been there for a long while. I came upon a doorway to my right. I peaked in that first room only to see a pile of rubbish in the center of the room. The rubbish was stacked with bricks, couple of old broken boards and some scattered electrical wires.

I left that room and went further up the hallway. The next room was to my left. It appeared to be the remnants of an old bathroom with a broken ceramic toilet and sink. Nothing too interesting in there so I moved on down the hallway even further. The next doorway I came to was also to my left. The stench of a rotting animal or wet animal hair or something made me semi gag for a half of a moment. I hesitated before going in there. I put my candle in front of me to light up the room a little before attempting entrance. I barely got my candle raised up when I suddenly felt something run across my foot. Of course it was the foot that had no shoe on it. I jumped back and screamed as I saw the shadows of a rat scurry off into the smelly room.

Having a rat run across my foot and the stench of rotten animal was enough for me to not venture any further and decided to return back to the familiar area of the Condo. Rather than going back into the Condo where Sunny was sleeping, I ventured outside to investigate the exterior part of the building; hopefully encountering less rat activity.

Back outside, I remembered to put the board back up from the opening that I came from. The weather was still muggy but not yet raining. I walked to the side of the building towards the street. Next to the building was a bunch of scattered garbage. There were several broken beer bottles, a weathered plastic grocery sack, some tin foil that appeared to be molded into a make shift crack pipe and I think there was something that looked like a used condom but didn't want get close enough to validate its authenticity.

Out on the street, I walked down to the intersection of the crossing streets. Standing on the corner I contemplated if I should flag down a policeman, go to the police station, go to the hospital or what exactly. All I knew is that I just needed to tell someone or somebody that I couldn't remember anything and that I needed some help. I was standing there thinking about my options when I noticed a middle aged woman was soon to walk past me.

"Excuse, me," I said to the woman to get her attention. "I was wondering if you could help me out."

Before I had a chance to ask her where the nearest hospital or nearest police station was she quickly replied shaking her hand in the air with an 'oh snap' attitude. "Get a job loser! I work hard for my money and I aint gonna give it out to people like you who only snort it up their nose; and while you're at it, take a bath!" She turned on her heel and walked off.

I stood there jaw dropped at her rudeness. She must think I am a homeless vagrant begging for money. I looked down at my clothes. I was dirty and understood why she must have thought that of me. I woke up in that pile of garbage and then spent the last few days in sweat and dirty blankets. I did smell. I wanted to scream back at the rude lady and tell her that I would love to take a bath but I don't have that convenience like you, you snooty bitch! But I didn't, I just stood there and took it; hurt from her harsh words.

I was about to go further down to the next block but before I did, a car drove by and flung a bunch of change at me, only to have one of the heavier coins hitting me in my right eye. I bent over in pain and quickly covered my eye with my hand for a few seconds until the pain eased up. When the pain subsided, I removed my hand and blinked my eye a few times until my vision came back into focus. I got down on my hands and knees to pick up the loose change that was strewn about on the sidewalk around me. If anything, I could us the coins to make a phone call to someone of authority for help.

I was down on my hands and knees picking up the coins, when two boys came trolling by me on their bikes. As they rode by me, one of the boys ran over my finger tips on my left hand. They both sped away before the one boy turned his head back to laugh and mock me as I screamed out from the pain. With the boy's snide mockery, I realized he must have run over my hand on purpose.

I shook my fingers back and forth to alleviate the pain of the tire skid marks on my fingers, only to realize my feelings were more bruised and hurt from the mean and rude behavior that was directed to me in those few minutes on the street corner. I decided that I had enough. Being in that dark building and having rats crawl over my foot was less emotionally painful than the cruel world outside. Finding help would have to wait for another time and day.

It was as I was walking back to the safety of the Condo when the skies above me spewed its anger at me beating out any remaining pride I had left in me. Heavy rain pelted my body, stinging my skin and soaking me to the core. The raindrops soon blended with my tears that were falling from my cheeks so that no one could see me cry.

I fell to my knees and cried even harder. I was broken. The cruel world around me finally broke my soul and any pride and energy I possibly had left in me. Everything was taken from me. I didn't know who I was, I was raped and living in a dirty, dark and musty, rat infested building. I was now yelled at, tortured with coins and run over by tires and laughed at by young boys. I had one shoe and a shirt with a broken strap. Now I was wet and worst yet, I still smelled!

Struggling my way back to the Condo, I stripped myself of my wet clothes, laid down on the dirty blankets while keeping one of the dirty sweat soaked blankets on top of me. Destroyed and lost, I cried myself to sleep for the rest of the day and into the night.

My night was restless. I was in and out of dreams all night long. The last dream I had was that I was awake but I couldn't move. Something or someone was holding me down. Out of nowhere I saw a puff of billowy smoke rise up from my body. In my dream I realized that I must have died and my spirit was leaving me. I screamed: "No, no, I don't want to die." I think I was yelling out loud when I suddenly woke up. Just like the other morning, I woke up again in a cold and clammy sweat. This time, it wasn't from the fever but from the fear of my nightmares.

CHAPTER FOUR

The following morning was upon me as the sun was cracking through the small window. The sun was in full shine without a cloud in the sky. The depressive atmosphere had dissipated; if for a while anyway. Today was a new day. I was outside after relieving my bladder when Sunny came up to do the same. I was leaning up against the building feeling well rested and trying to enjoy the morning briskness of the morning when Sunny soon joined me against the building.

"I cannot believe we both slept all day yesterday and all last night too," I stated in disbelief that we both slept for such a long time. "I suppose since I was ill, I needed more sleep but why in the world did you sleep for that length of time?" I asked with curiosity.

"I do that all the time, exclaimed Sunny. "There are times when I don't sleep for three or four days. After that many days awake, it all catches up to me and then sometimes I end up sleeping for a couple of days straight. It's more normal for me than you think," she replied.

We exchanged some more small talk and after a few minutes, Sunny suggested that we make a trip down to one of the homeless shelters to get a pair of shoes for me and perhaps a free lunch.

"How far away is it?" I asked

"It's about a mile away from here. The Mormons run it. The Mormons are quite active around here and try to save us all from the evils of life."

Even though the pain in my crotch and head was still a little present, it was much less. I was feeling better and believed I could pretty easily make the mile journey but now I was more concerned if I would make it all that way barefoot on the cement sidewalks making my feet raw as hamburger. Regardless, I had to go as I really needed some shoes. I certainly couldn't walk around barefoot forever.

Actually, the idea of doing something other than hanging around the Condo would be an uplifting activity and possibly help my depressed demeanor. It would also be nice to venture out with someone who knew their way around this area.

"Do you think I could get some Tylenol or Motrin or something like that at the Shelter?" I asked.

"Nah, they don't give out medication or drugs of any kind, but we can do some spanging today to get some money if you want. Then you can buy some yourself."

"Spanging? What is spanging?" I asked inquisitively.

She started laughing as she shook her head back and forth in jest, "Girlfriend, are you for real? Come on Missy, I'll show you the way."

We barely started walking when I heard a witty musical tone. Sunny pulled out a cell phone and started talking. I wondered how someone could be homeless, yet have money for a cellular phone. I overheard her talking to someone about scoring ten balloons and where to meet later today. It didn't take me long to figure out she was talking about some type of street drug harder than just a one-hitter of some pot. Sunny must have seen the concerned look on my face and soon hung up.

"You smoke, snort or shoot?" she asked.

"I don't think so. I mean, not that I can remember and I am not really interested in doing any drugs right now anyway."

"That's cool. No reason to start up now." She gave me a little shoulder bump and smiled...subliminally telling me all was amiable between us. On the way to the Shelter she filled me in on her life which was quite unlike what I expected. She had a college degree in Computer Programming and worked for IBM in Chicago.

"I was married and had two little girls; Emily and Olivia," she said with the most satisfying smile that she could endure.

"Had?" I asked.

She went on to tell me that she got into drinking and drugs in college. After Olivia, her second child, was born her addictions took control of her life. Her husband eventually divorced her and got custody of her girls. Shortly thereafter, she lost her job at IBM and was unable to hold down any other jobs due to her drug addiction.

"I was so sad when I lost my girls. They were the most important thing in my life. I was really fucked up emotionally and my thoughts were all distorted. I knew it wouldn't be much longer before I lost my job."

She paused for a moment before she went on, "This sounds harsh or cold but it was almost worse losing my job than losing custody of my girls. I mean, it gave me comfort knowing my girls would be safe with my ex-husband so once I lost my job; it was almost as if I was given a free pass in life to give up and go off the deep end. I didn't care about anything. I just went crazy. I drank, snorted, shot up anything and everything I could get my hands on. I didn't care if I lived or died. I ended up in the hospital about four times and was court ordered to go to treatment once. I lasted about three days in the treatment center. It was a bullshit place so I decided to get out of there and hitch a ride to California; you know, get out of the cold weather. I made it to Salt Lake City and haven't quite made it to California. I have been here two years now."

I didn't say anything as I didn't know what to say. I just listened to her story and nodded as she was talking. We walked in silence for a few moments before she spoke quietly as she looked down.

"Someday, I will see my girls again and get them back." She looked off and over the horizon and proceeded on, "There's not a day goes by that I don't think of them and miss them dearly. I just got to get enough money to get a bus ticket back there."

I stopped walking and turned to her. "You haven't accumulated enough money in two years to go back and see them?" I asked somewhat perplexed and a little sarcastic.

"It's harder than you think," she said in a soft and saddened voice and then kept walking forward to avoid any discussion on that subject.

I didn't know what to think of Sunny. I knew she was honest and forthcoming with her addictions and how it messed up her life. She wasn't candy coating anything or blaming someone else for her faults. For that, I trusted and appreciated her; however, I was sad for her, as she was quite intelligent and a nice person overall, not crazy like Aunt Bev or Bob the Magician. She was just an addict who gave up everything she loves for the need to get high.

Another block or so down the road, there was a big sign that said 'Pioneer Park'. I noticed a van parked next to a big pickup truck with a bunch of men gathered around a picnic table. A couple of them were sporting cowboy hats.

"I wonder what's going on over there." I questioned out loud, thinking maybe someone was in a fight or something. Sunny looked over to where I was pointing.

"Oh, ranch owners come into town this time of the year. They are looking for some men who are interested in working temporarily as ranch hands. The ranchers usually come around this area as they are able to easily hire temporary help since there are a large number of jobless people around this area who need the money and don't expect health insurance, 401k's and all of that crap. The ranchers have to come here as most don't have phones to contact them or transportation to get to the ranch. The men come to the park in hopes to get hired since it is only a temporary job to get some extra income; however, most of them are repeats.

"Why do they do that this time of the year, ya know, in the early spring?"

"Well, I've heard the ranchers are in need of extra help because in the springtime, they are busy tilling the fields, planting and fertilizing their crops. In the meantime, all the cows are calving and they need extra people to monitor their herds to assure the calves are safe from coyotes and other types of predators. I guess they usually do other stuff too like repair fences, paint buildings and miscellaneous stuff like that after the winter has taken a toll on their ranches."

"Have you ever gone to a ranch to work?"

"Are you crazy girlfriend? Hell no!"

"Do they just hire men or do they hire women too?" I asked, again finding that process rather intriguing.

"I don't know but rumor has it that they work you to death. I suppose it is good money, but I know I would never last."

I wondered if it was too hard of work for her or if she knows she wouldn't have readily access to her drugs.

It seems we had walked about a mile or so when out of nowhere Sunny picked up a glass beer bottle. As she did, she shoved us both behind the next building. She put her finger up to her lips as if she was informing me to be quiet. She then took the beer bottle by the neck and wrapped my broom skirt around the bottle before lightly tapping it against the brick wall behind us. I heard the muffled sounds of the beer bottle breaking.

I had no idea of what she was doing, other than I knew not to question her or make a sound of any kind. I just stood there and leaned against the side of the building where she motioned me to stay.

With the broken beer bottle in her hand she took a stance next to the edge of the building by the sidewalk. A skanky pot bellied man around fifty years old came around the corner to where we were standing. As he did and before he had a chance to do or say anything, Sunny grabbed him by the back of his hair and stuck the broken bottle up to his neck saying, "One fucking move and I will cut your neck and leave you to die back here for the rats to feed off your fat pathetic body."

The man, in total surprise said, "Whoa, whoa, no problem here, just walking along enjoying the day." He lifted his hands up in the air as if he was surrendering.

"You ever think of coming near me or my friend again, you will be one sorry mother fucker. You understand compadre?"

The man shook his head up and down in agreement as Sunny slowly removed the grasp she had of his hair but leaving the bottle close to his neck.

The pot bellied man took a few steps backward away from Sunny saying "You ladies have a nice day." As he was telling us to have a nice day, he put his hands back down and proceeded to zip up his fly. I never noticed the zipper of his pants was down until then. The man started to walk back the way he came from. When he was far enough away, Sunny turned back to me where I was standing in total shock and awe. I stood there wide-eyed at the whole ordeal. I didn't have time be afraid, I was just dumbfounded.

"That fucking perv," Sunny stated as she walked back towards me.

"Oh my God Sunny, who was that guy and what just happened?" I asked.

"Didn't you see him following us since the park?" she asked.

"No, no I didn't."

"I have seen that guy around plenty of times beating himself off or showing his dick to me or other people. I needed to give him a message that you don't want to fuck with me," she stated angrily.

I didn't know if I should have thanked Sunny, cheered, cried or screamed. That whole episode showed me, from that point on, that Sunny would have my back and I would be safe when I was with her.

"Come on, we only have a couple of blocks left," as she grabbed me again by my arm. "Fucking perv," she whispered again under her breath as we continued walking.

By the time we got to the homeless shelter, my feet were hot and sore but I surprisingly made it. We were greeted by a kind and gray haired gentleman. He knew Sunny and asked how she was doing. After they were done catching up, he sent us to a room that was filled with clothes and other miscellaneous items that people could take free of charge. I picked out a pair of white and pink tennis shoes that seems to fit fairly well along with a pair of white ankle socks. I eyed up a backpack which I thought would be useful to carry my clothes in and then continued to dig through the piles of clothes. I found a couple of pair of underwear that looked fairly new, an oversized T-shirt to sleep in, a hoodie and a pair of black stretch pants as well as another tank top since the strap was broken on the top that I had.

My back pack was now full but I did manage to find a scarf and a hairbrush and shoved them in there for good measure. From there I went to the bathroom and gave myself a quick sponge bath. The smell of soap was the best smell right now. I washed the stink off most of my upper torso. I brushed my hair and when I did, a few clumps of dried blood fell into the sink next to me. My hair was greasy and dirty so I stuck my head under the faucet to give my scalp and hair a quick rinse. Since my hair was wet, I took the scarf and wrapped it around my head and tied it into a cute bow in front. Not ideal, but it would do until I could get into to a bath or shower. I put on my new-used clothes and threw my top with the broken strap and my one sandal in the garbage pail that was under the sink.

After cleaning up and donning some clean clothes, I felt like a new human being. I had a 'giddy up' in my step and my attitude. It is amazing what a sponge bath and some new clothes will do for a person. As I was looking in the mirror admiring myself, Sunny knocked on the door.

"Are you almost done? I am starving!" After she said that, I realized how hungry I was as well and opened the bathroom door only to see Sunny there patiently waiting for me.

"Wow, you clean up pretty good," she exclaimed. "I hardly would have recognized you. You look like a completely different person!"

I thanked Sunny and we both went to the dining area where we were greeted by a set of other workers. They were all so calm and had a peaceful aura about them. They were very non-confronting, unlike the world I just came from outside of the homeless shelters four walls.

Even though it was only 10:30 in the morning, the volunteer workers warmed up some soup for us. Along with the soup, they gave us some bread, milk and cake. I didn't realize how famished I was and the hot soup seemed to warm my soul. We both ate until our stomachs hurt.

After we were done eating, we went out back to the dumpster to look for some cardboard boxes. Sunny informed me that we each need a large piece of cardboard, which we quickly found. She showed me how we have to print large letters in black magic marker (which she retrieved from the shelter while I was picking over the clothes) so that people can easily read the signs. She made sure we put "God Bless" on our signs since people tend to give you more when they know you believe in God, especially since this is a highly populated area with the Mormon religion.

Once we got our cardboard signs made, she started to educate me some more. "The location and time of the day are the most important things. It's best if you go around the lunch hour and after work, somewhere between eleven and two P.M. and again between four and seven P.M. as those times are the busiest and you'll get a better opportunity for money; you know, more money for less time in the hot sun. You also have to go on a corner where there is a stop light or a stop sign."

"Why is that?" I asked inquisitively.

"It is because people have to stop. When they stop and you are standing next to their car, they are more likely to hand over some money as they feel uncomfortable or guilty for not giving you anything. So, they give what they have to clear their conscious. It is no sense in standing on a street where cars don't stop. Especially if it a busy street, they won't stop to hand over money because even if they truly wanted to give you some money, they wouldn't stop to give you any as they would interrupt the flow of traffic and possibly cause an accident. They just won't risk that."

"That makes a lot of sense," as I nodded my head in understanding.

Sunny continued on, "So once you find your corner with a stop light, then you walk along the stopped cars. They won't get out of their cars to give you money but if you walk up to their cars, they will usually give you something."

"Wow, amazing." I just never realized there was such planning in begging for money.

"Do you do this a lot? I mean...is this how you make your money for stuff?"

"No," she stated without any further explanation. "It's not always money. Sometimes people will offer you food, clothes and other opportunities for extra cash."

"Like jobs and stuff?"

"Ya, you could call it that," she said matter-of-factly. So are you ready then?"

"Sure."

"For today only, we will do this together and we can split the money but after today, we need to do this separately. If we are different spots we can each make our own money, ya know, twice as much. Oh one last thing. If you see or suspect any type of a law enforcement officers, turn and walk away as fast as you can as they frown on spanging in this town."

"Got it," I replied hoping that no one would throw money at me or yell at me to get a job. I was feeling too good today. I didn't want another day of emotional abuse. Feeling better, I knew I could handle it better today than yesterday morning but didn't want to be beaten down again by rude and mean people.

It was starting to get hot out when there was a break in the late noon rush hour traffic. I took that opportunity to sit down and drink a bottle of water that someone had given to me. I started to count my money and counted over twenty five dollars. I assume Sunny must have received about the same amount. Besides the money and the water, I was also given a one dollar coupon off a foot long at Subway, a book marker with a prayer verse on it and an energy drink that I had earlier drank.

After a short rest, and finishing my bottle of water, I saw Sunny up from me on the street. She was over a block from me catching the traffic coming from the other direction. I started walking towards her to let her know I was ready to call it quits. My feet were sore from walking so far and for so long, besides the fact that we had a mile walk back to our home base. Even though I had freshened up, got new clothes and was fed a decent meal, I was still recovering and my energy was starting to drain.

She was still a few steps ahead of me but before I could catch up to her to tell her that I was ready to go, a dark blue Cadillac pulled up to the stop sign next to her. A large man put his hand out the window to give Sunny some money. When Sunny reached for the money, I saw the man grab her hand and started talking to her. I saw her talk back to the man and nodded her head a few times. Fearing this was an undercover policeman, I hid my cardboard sign under my shirt to avoid any potential arrests. I watched the man pull away and park his car around the corner.

"Hey Missy," Sunny yelled at me as she motioned her hands to come over by her.

"I am going to go with this John for a drive and then meet up with a friend later today. Can you find your way back to the Condo without me?" she asked.

"Um, ya I think so," I replied hesitantly thinking about the perv that was following us earlier this morning.

"That's my girl."

"Do you know that guy in the Cadillac?" I asked wondering why she willingly would go with a stranger without knowing him.

"Wow, seriously Missy? How naïve are you?" she stated mockingly. "I can make more money in ten minutes with this dude than what we made out here spanging for the last couple of hours. I can be in a nice cool area and be off my feet at the same time," she stated as she gave me a wink.

Shocked at what she was doing, we quickly divided up our money. I started back to the Condo alone wondering why she would be willing to go with this unknown man who paid her for sex verses cutting up a fat man who beat himself off in front of her. What was the difference? In my mind they were both perverted in some way. I guess the only difference is the one guy was willing to pay for a sexual encounter and the other guy was just a sick person wanting to get a rise from someone else's reaction from showing his penis. I suppose that makes him more of a pervert.

On the way home, I stopped at the nearby convenience store and bought a small bottle of Tylenol, a toothbrush and some toothpaste. I still had a couple bucks left over, so I bought a granola bar for something to eat later tonight. I also bought a glass bottle of root beer with a long neck on it. If I didn't need the soda bottle for a weapon on the walk home, I can drink it later or give it to Bob the Magician or Aunt Bev as a nice gesture.

I woke up the next morning and realized I was drooling from sleeping so hard. I don't think I budged or moved all night. All the walking to the shelter and back, the fresh air and sun that I received from the spanging yesterday and the dose of Tylenol, made sleep like a rock. I sat up and stretched for a few minutes and looked around. Aunt Bev was gone and most likely out scavenging the streets for food or other miscellaneous treasures. Bob the Magician was off in a corner giving a magic show to an imaginary audience.

I donned my clothes, tennis shoes and wrapped my scarf around my greasy hair before going outside to pee. I gave a glance over at Sunny's bed noticing that she was there and that she made it home safe and sound after her encounter with that man in the blue Cadillac. Walking closer by her bed, I smelled something foul. I looked over and saw vomit next to her. It was in her bedding and in her hair. Before going outside, I decided to wake her up and bring her outside with me to get some fresh air and possibly go get some water to clean herself as well as her bed, as the smell was overwhelming.

"Sunny," I said in a loud voice hoping that would wake her from her drunken or high stupor. I didn't want to get any closer to that vomit smell than I had to. When she didn't respond, I took a big breath and held it before I walked up to her. I called out her name again and shook her on the shoulder. When I did, her shoulder she was ice cold. In shock, I gasped and pulled my hand back afraid of her coldness. Some of her hair was over her face and the rest of her body was covered up by a blanket.

I stood there for a second or two wondering what I should do. I shook her harder and when I did, her body rolled over. Her lips were white and her eyes were half open staring into space. I looked down and saw a loose rubber strap around her left arm and a needle lying next to the puddle of vomit.

I was so shocked and scared that I started to scream. I put my hand over my mouth as I started to shake with fright. It wasn't long before Bob the Magician heard my screams and ran over to my side next to Sunny's bed, only to see the same horrid scene that was before us.

"Lordy, Lordy. My, my, my. Dear Sunny Delight, you's sure's gone and done it dis time," he stated as he shook his head back and forth.

We both just sat there and stared at her knowing she was dead. I was whimpering to myself and half gagging from the sight and the smell of the vomit.

"I never saw a dead person before," I whispered as if I was not supposed to talk aloud.

"We's gunna have to carry her on outta here," said Bob the Magician

"What?" I turned and looked at him with dismay.

"We can't have no police in here. They'll make us leave and then we's won't have no's other place to go. No sirs, we can't have no police in here."

I looked at him with disbelief. Was he seriously thinking that we couldn't call the police when someone has just died? His thinking was distorted and wrong. "We cannot just throw her out in the street like a bag of garbage!" I screamed.

"No ma'am, we's gotta take her outta here, and that's that," he said in disagreement.

I felt myself gloss over in disbelief as to how absurd his thought process was. In fact, this whole thing is wrong…this whole lifestyle of living in this squalor, begging for money, and hanging out with crazy people who talk to themselves, drug addict prostitutes and walking around with glass bottles for weapons. All of this, it wasn't me or who I am.

I felt myself start to hyperventilate and needed to get out of this dark and volatile place where I didn't belong. I grabbed my backpack and ran outside to the sunlight. I ran down the block, not really knowing where I was heading and not having a particular place to go. I just had to get away from the craziness that was around me. I knew this is not what I was about or made of, so I just ran afraid and fighting my own tears.

It was just a few minutes later when I realized I was back at Pioneer Park; the park where the cowboys were yesterday. They were still there today. I ran over there just as a clean cut cowboy was getting up from the picnic bench.

"Wait, wait. I want to go work on the ranch," I screamed desperately.

The cowboy turned to me and gave me the once over. "I am sorry ma'am but I just finished interviewing and hiring all the hired hands we needed and was just about to head out with them."

"Please, you have to take me. I will work very hard for you, I promise!" By this time I was pleading for him to take me.

He could see that I was distraught and said, "Are you in trouble with the law or something because we don't take felons, criminal, drug addicts or anyone else of that type? We do a full back ground check on everyone."

"No, no, I am not a drug addict and I am not running from the law, I just want to get out of here and do some real work for some real money."

For some reason, he must have took pity on me as he squinted his eyes and gave me the once over one more time before he said, "Well maybe we could find something for you."

"Thank you, thank you," I replied. "I won't let you down."

"Fill out this paper with the needed information. We are heading out at ten am." He looked at his watch and then said, "Which is in about five minutes."

"That's fine; I have everything I need in this bag."

He handed me the paper which had about four blanks to fill in: Full Name, Address, Social Security Number, Emergency Contact Name and Number. I started to fill in my name but didn't know my middle name so I just put down Missy McDonalds and left the middle name blank. If he asks, I will make up something. I was stumped for a minute regarding what address to enter, but then I remembered the address to the homeless shelter that Sunny and I went to yesterday. When it came to my Social Security number, I just quickly wrote down some numbers without even thinking about it too much. I just left the emergency contact blank. If he asks, I will tell him that I am alone and have no family. When I was done filling out the paper, I handed it over to the cowboy.

"The van is full so you will have to ride with me in my truck. I hope you don't mind."

"No, no, that is fine," I answered jumping in the big diesel pickup, thankful that I cleaned the stench from my body yesterday at the shelter.

As we drove off, my thoughts quickly drifted back to Sunny. I knew that Bob the Magician and Aunt Bev would not be able to carry her out together since dead weight can be quite heavy. The police will have to come in and get her. I wondered if the police will trace her back to her family and daughters in Chicago so they know what had happened to her. It was sad…the whole thing was just sad yet I was so thankful to not have to live that lifestyle any longer; for now anyway.

My thoughts also brought me to Aunt Bev and how I left the Condo without getting a chance to thank her for taking care of me and how grateful I was for her nursing me back to health. Would I be alive today without her help? By this time, I could feel some tears now starting to well up in my eyes thinking of all the crazy and emotionally draining things that have happened in the last few days but held them in so that the cowboy wouldn't see me cry. I was glad that whole ordeal of living on the street was over. I was happy I was in this truck yet nervous about working at the ranch and what will become of me there.

Life Three

CHAPTER FIVE

Once we got on the outskirts of town, the cowboy spoke up, "My name is Sheldon Parker. My brother Jason and I own and run the Parker Ranch. It has been in our family for over 50 years. I have a wife Miriam and two kids, Jack who is twelve and Lindsay, who just turned fifteen. We live in the main house on the Ranch. My brother Jason, who is driving the van, lives in the smaller house on the opposite side of the Ranch. He is divorced and his daughter Savannah visits for a few weeks here and there over the summer as well as Christmas and other holidays, so you won't see much of her."

"Jason's ex-wife must have moved far away since she doesn't come on weekends like most children of divorce?"

"California. His ex didn't like the country ranch life. She also has family back in California that she can be with. She and Jason have been divorced for about four or five years now. I am glad she left. She was a real condescending witch…excuse my language."

"No offense taken," I grinned, amused at his candor.

"We hire about ten extras this time of the year but this year we hired fourteen, well...fifteen including you. We hired the extra hands this year because a few typically end up quitting before the first week is over. They don't like to exert themselves very hard on manual labor and cannot hack working every day of the week; even if it is temporary."

I wasn't sure if he was feeling me out for how hard I was going to work or my thoughts on hard work. "You don't have to worry about me. I am a good worker and am really organized. I won't let you down." After I said that, I wondered why I did say that. I don't know if I am a good employee or well organized, but I must be. I said it without thinking as if I said it a million times before as if I knew those were good qualities that I have. This made me think how long it will be before I remember anything else.

"Good, glad to hear that. I am going to have you start out with Javier and Felicia in the kitchen and laundry. They are our cooks and also do the basic laundry. With the extra hired hands this spring, they will probably need a little extra help. I will be checking in with them every day or so to see if you are needed for the whole day or not. If not, we can find something for you, even if it is helping my wife out around our house with the kids. Remember, this is only temporary, we may only need you for one week or maybe more; no guarantees."

"I understand," I replied just thankful I was getting out of the street living.

It was about an hour and a half before we finally turned onto a dirt road. There was a huge wooden sign that had an engraving of a couple of cows on the sign with the words: 'Parker Ranch'.

We drove up a long driveway and finally came upon an area with numerous buildings. I saw the two houses that Sheldon told me about earlier. Off to the side were a couple of barns and about three large tin buildings where they probably store their equipment. To the right were three smaller log cabin types of houses and another very large log cabin looking building in the center of them all.

As we were pulling up, Sheldon stated, "Jason is in charge of the ranch hands. He assigns the jobs and orients them to their designated duties. He also assigns the workers to their bunkhouses and beds. All the ranch hands stay in the bunkhouses except for Javier and Felicia, they stay in the lodge; that big cabin over there," he said nodding his head in the direction of the largest log building in the center of the bunkhouses.

"Javier and Felicia have been with us for about five years now. They are married and live here about six months in the spring, summer and fall and then go back to Mexico City the other six months during the winter season as they have family back there.

"You will have you stay in the lodge as well. The lodge is where the kitchen and dining area is located as well as the laundry. There is a small room in back where Javier and Felicia stay, but there is another small empty room behind the laundry that we converted into a small sleeping room last year. I think you will be comfortable there."

We walked in together towards the lodge when we were greeted by a very furry and very fat dog. Its tail was wagging and its rear end was swaying back and forth so hard that I thought it would dislocate its back. I am not familiar with dog breeds but is probably a mix of shepherd and maybe collie or golden retriever since it had so much fur.

"This is Molly."

"Hello Molly," I said as I scratched her ears and the back of her neck. "Aren't you a healthy and happy dog?" I exclaimed. Molly reciprocated by nudging her body close to mine showing me she enjoyed the scratching and attention.

"Molly stays in the three sided lean-to in back of the lodge next to where the garbage bins are kept; you'll see that later. Javier feeds her and makes sure she has water."

"Well, I should be able to handle that," I stated trying to make humor out of my unknown future.

We walked into the lodge and I saw a short little Mexican man with an apron on making some flour tortillas in the kitchen. He must have heard us come in as he turned to us and smiled. "Senior Sheldon" he exclaimed with his Mexican accent. "What brings you to my kitchen?"

"Javier, this is Missy, I am going to have her help you and Felicia out in the kitchen and the laundry for a few weeks or maybe more."

"Oh, I am so happy to get some extra help," replied Javier and then turned his direction to me. "I would shake your hand but my hands are full of flour."

"That's just fine. Nice to meet you Javier," acknowledging his greeting.

"Is Felicia around?" Sheldon asked.

"She is resting right now, but I will bring her out later when she is awake."

"How is she feeling lately?"

"She tires easily and seems to get weaker every day, so again, thank you for the extra help." Javier turned his attention to me and stated, "Felicia used to help me with the kitchen work and the laundry but she has been ailing so bad that she is not much help anymore. She has Multiple Sclerosis and it is getting worse. At this point, she can only fold the linens as the kitchen work is just too much for her."

"I am sorry to hear that Javier," I replied. There was an uncomfortable silence for a few seconds before Sheldon spoke up.

"I am going to go ahead and give Missy a quick tour and then I will send her out to help you."

Javier nodded again, "Gracias. Gracias Senior Sheldon."

Sheldon showed me where the phone was kept that had a list of phone numbers tacked up next to it. The numbers included the main house to reach him and Miriam, as well as each of their cells phones. The cell numbers of his brother Jason, and Tommy, the Parkers full time hired hand. Also on the list were the typical emergency numbers, such as poison control, and etc.

We moved on to the laundry room where there were two front load washers and two dryers. Beside them was a small table that held the laundry soap and fabric softener. On the opposite side of the room were two gray dumpsters; one labeled: "LINENS/TOWELS" and the other labeled "PERSONAL". White linens, towels and washcloths were neatly folded and kept on the adjacent shelves.

Sheldon led me through a door in back of the laundry room which entered to a back hallway. Across the hall to the right was Javier and Felicia's room and to the left was my room. It was tiny but had enough room for a twin bed, a bedside stand with a digital clock on it, and even had a very tiny closet big enough to hold a couple pieces of clothing and a couple pair of shoes. I had to hold in my emotions as it was a room with four walls, a real bed with a box spring and mattress that had bed sheets and clean blankets on it.

"Around the corner and over here is the bathroom and shower. You will have to share with Javier and Felicia."

I didn't care if I had to share it with Ted Bundy. It had a toilet and a shower and a sink and a door for privacy.

"You go ahead and settle in and then go check in with Javier and he can orientate you to your duties."

"Thanks again Sheldon, I won't let you and Jason down. I promise."

It took about thirty seconds to unpack since I didn't have anything. I wanted to shower but thought it best to get out and help Javier as soon as possible. I didn't want to start out by being late and upsetting Javier so I just washed up and headed out for the first day of my new job.

When I returned to the kitchen, Javier was no longer full of flour and was just cleaning up his mess. He smiled when I walked in the room.

"Oh, the Parkers are so very good to work for," he said. "You are very lucky. They have treated Felicia and I like family from the first day we came here."

"That's good," thinking about the fact that I don't have a family of my own, that I know of anyway.

"Jason, Tommy and the ranch hands come in for breakfast between 6:30 and 7:00 a.m., lunch between 12:00 and 12:30, and supper between 6:30 and 7:00 p.m. Sheldon mostly eats breakfast and supper with his family up at the house but sometimes he will eat here if his wife is out with the kids or something like that."

Javier was no stranger to giving directions as to what I should do, so I dove right in with my new duties of helping prepare the supper meal.

It was close to six o'clock that evening when Jason and the ranch hands randomly started to come through the dining hall doors and sit down at the tables. Some were laughing, some were quiet and some were just talking about dealing with the cattle or ranch related business as they began to eat. It was then that a specific ranch hand caught my eye as he entered the dining hall. He was a tall with wide shoulders and darker skin as if he was Alaskan or Native American Indian. He had high cheek bones with deep set dark eyes.

Before sitting at a table, he hung his cowboy hat on a rack that was mounted on the wall next to the door. When he took off his hat, I could see he had long black hair pulled back in a pony tail, which made me think he was most likely Native. He then proceeded to wash and dry his hands at the nearby sink before walking to the table nearest to the kitchen area. His walk was strong and rhythmic, as if he had a purpose. He didn't say a word. He just gave a simple nod of recognition to the others as he walked by them. When he sat down, he bowed his head and prayed silently to himself before he began to eat.

I was in awe of this man for some reason and I watched him as he ate his meal. He took the time to wipe his mouth with the napkin that was in his lap; unlike some of the others who were using their shirt sleeves to clean themselves. When supper was over, he put his silverware across the plate indicating he was done; again unlike the others who just left everything there and walked out. He slowly got up, methodically walked back to the sink, rinsed and dried his hands again, put his cowboy hat back on and silently walked outside.

I was suddenly brought from my trance when Javier started to bark orders at me again. "Okay, now we get the plates from the tables and clean up."

After several trips back and forth carrying dirty dishes from the tables to the kitchen, twenty minutes had passed. By the time we actually got done washing all the dishes and putting leftovers in containers, another hour was gone...and that was with two of us working at it. I barely sat down to get a drink of water when Javier said, "Now we have to get a few things ready for breakfast and boxed lunches for those who won't be here for lunch and out in the range. They need to take their lunches with them."

"How many take their lunches with them?" I asked.

"There are two ranch hands that rotate twelve hour shifts. They watch over the cattle that are grazing and are too far out on the range for them to come back for every meal. They have capabilities to warm food up over fires so those two ranchers are exceptions to the rest. You always have meals made up for them in advance, which are usually leftovers from the main meals. As far as the others and how many box lunches you need for them depends on what they are doing and if they will be close enough to eat lunch here. Typically, I make about seven or so lunches. If there are a few extras, Felicia and I will eat them for our lunch or if it is something that can sit an extra day just save it for the next day. If there isn't enough, I just quickly set up another one or two, depending on how many are needed."

When we were done making lunches for the next day, Javier took the time to show me around in the kitchen area. There were two refrigerators, a huge walk in food pantry and a fairly good sized walk in freezer. He showed me where he kept his two week meal plan schedule and where he kept the list for groceries. I looked over his food menu and noticed that most of his meal choices were Mexican oriented dishes; tortilla soup, enchiladas, and burritos of sort. I saw that he did have fish on the menu for one evening supper, only to follow it with fish tacos for lunch the next day. I thought to myself that my brothers would never go for that kind of food on a regular basis. They would want hardy food such as meat, potatoes and gravy.

Oh my God. I just realized that I have brothers. I said brother's meaning more than one. How many do I have? I couldn't remember. Brothers! I have brothers! Some of my memory is coming back.

Before I had a chance to make sense of my new found recollection, I was brought back to reality when I heard Javier say, "Miriam, Sheldon's wife, goes into town every Wednesday morning at 8:00am to get supplies, so make sure you have your grocery list and any personal things you need and have it ready for her before then."

"Its 9:00pm now, when do you have time do all the laundry on top of all this food preparing, serving and clean up?"

"Felicia would usually do the laundry after the morning meals a couple days of the week. Jason and Sheldon have an All Terrain Vehicle (ATV) in front of the lodge that we are allowed to use. Usually Felicia would use it and drive to the bunk houses. At each bunk house, she would strip the bed sheets and collect all the dirty towels and washcloths. Then, she would restock the bunk houses with fresh linens and towels for the rest of the week. If the ranchers want their personal laundry washed they are to have it in the laundry baskets in their bunk houses. Felicia gathers the clothes in the baskets at that same time. If the clothes are not in the laundry basket, we leave them there. We don't want to be taking something that we shouldn't with their personal belongings. Anyway, Felicia would do this but lately I have had to do that too since she has been getting so weak. I do that on Sundays as Sundays are typically a little lighter here in the kitchen."

"Why are Sunday's lighter?" I asked.

"After breakfast, I am supposed to have the rest of the day off, so I usually make everyone a packed lunch and then a hearty soup with tortillas for their supper. They come in at their own convenience and serve themselves. Miriam and the kids come down in the evening and clean up the kitchen so that we are able to have some time off for ourselves, but I usually end up doing it anyway, as I have to come in and prepare for the next days breakfast. It is a lot lighter but we don't really get a day off," he said as he shook his head. He appeared tired and worn out. I did feel sorry for him but thought I would still rather do this than sleep in a dark ransacked building, peeing outside and begging for money.

"Thank you for your help today Missy, now I am going to go to bring a late supper plate to Felicia and then get ready for bed myself. I already told you that they start coming in for breakfast between 6:30 to 7:00am so we need to be down here by 5:30am."

"Yes, you are welcome. I am bushed myself. I am not used to working so hard."

"Good night then and I will see you in the morning," he replied as he turned to walk back to his room located in back of the kitchen area.

I took a long hot shower, thinking that was the first time I had a real shower since I can remember, which was when I woke up by the dumpster. I closed my eyes and let the warm droplets warm my skin and sooth my soul at the same time. I never realized how good soap and shampoo smelled. The warmth, the smell was not only refreshing but therapeutic for my body and mind.

I was so thankful that Sheldon was willing to bring me here. I crawled into bed that night smelling the freshness of the linens while trying to fester up any other memories of my brothers. I know I have brothers...meaning more than one. It seems like I had three but I couldn't be sure. I tried to recall anything but it seemed to be all blank. I am in hopes that I will remember more as days progress by but for now, I thought it best to try and get some sleep. I need to get up early to help prepare for the next morning's breakfast.

CHAPTER SIX

It was Monday, midmorning and a couple of days after my arrival. I was in the kitchen with Javier shredding some beef that he had slow cooked throughout the night, when Sheldon came walking into the kitchen area.

"Senior Sheldon, I suppose you are here to check up on Missy. I must say, she is doing an excellent job!"

"Good Javier, I am glad to hear that," replied Sheldon acknowledging his praise. "Missy, may I have a word with you in private?"

"Sure," I said concerned about his request. I left Javier and Sheldon and I went to the furthest table from the kitchen prep area for more privacy before sitting down.

"As I mentioned in the truck the other day, the day I hired you, that we do a background check on all of our hires. The Social Security number that you provided did not come back as Missy McDonalds but another name of a female in another State." He was silent waiting for a reaction which left me feeling vulnerable and uncomfortable to the silence.

I knew this trick when I worked corporate. When you want information from another person who is not really forthcoming, all you do is make a statement or ask a question about the issue and then stare at them without saying anything else. You are purposely leaving the other person hanging there. The other person feels very uncomfortable from the silence and they start to talk about anything to avoid the awkward of the silence. Reporters often do this, as well as the police to get people to talk. Incidentally, they confess or spill the beans to the issue at hand, whatever it may be. It was then I realized another memory fact came to me in my conversation with Sheldon. I must have worked at a high level corporate job, but now was not the time to deal with that. All I could do was to acknowledge his findings.

"Yes. I am sorry Sheldon. You are right." I looked down in shame, "I don't have a confirmatory response for you other than the fact that you will have to trust me when I say I am not a criminal."

He was silent again for a moment as if he was thinking or considering his options before he finally spoke up. "I am sorry Missy, but you will have to go back with Miriam on Wednesday then. You may be running form someone or something but we expect full honesty supplemented with a confirmatory background on all of our hires; anything else would be misleading and we do not participate in any kind of fraudulent practices or support employees who are not forthcoming. We cannot have 'unknowns' around my family and those that we care about."

"Yes, I understand," I replied. "I will get my things ready to go. In the meantime, I will still help out Javier for my room and board until I have to leave."

He nodded as he stood up to leave.

"Sheldon?"

"Yes?"

"Take me seriously when I say that I do appreciate you and Jason for giving me this chance and opportunity. You made me feel like I was worthy and for that I am forever grateful."

"No problem," as he turned and walked out leaving me at the table saddened from the conversation.

I was heartbroken and sad and didn't want to go back to living on the street again. I wondered if Bob the Magician and Aunt Bev would take me back since I didn't help Bob the Magician take Sunny's dead body out with him. Then I wondered if they are still in the abandoned building or if the police kicked them out. Nevertheless, I knew when I got back to the city that I would have to make an honest attempt to find out who I am, regardless of what I find.

I went back to the kitchen not saying a word to Javier. Telling Javier that I was already leaving should be up to Jason or Sheldon.

I was abruptly awoken by a loud knock on my door. It took me a few times to recognize the noise because I was sleeping so soundly. I looked over at the bedside clock and it read 4:46am.

"Just a minute," I yelled as I sat up in bed blinking my eyes a few times. I stumbled to the door and opened it slightly, only to see Jason standing there with his cowboy hat in his hands.

"I am sorry to wake you Missy but I had to take Javier and Felicia to the airport earlier tonight. They got word that his son was in a horrible car accident in Mexico City and they were not sure if he was going to make it through the next 24 hours. I just got back now."

I gasped in shock, "Oh no, that is horrible!"

"Yes ma'am. We will all have to say a prayer for them. Um, I know this is a lot to ask but I was hoping that you would be willing and able to run breakfast by yourself this morning? Did Javier show you around enough so that you can do it by yourself?"

"Yes, yes of course. Under the circumstances it will have to work, no matter what. If push comes to shove, they can eat cereal if need be," I said assuring.

"Ok then, I will talk to you more after breakfast and thank you again," he stated as he turned and walked away putting his cowboy hat back on.

I was just finishing cleaning up the kitchen after the morning breakfast rush when Sheldon came into the dining hall. "Missy, do you have a moment?

I dried my hands on a towel. "Well, I made it through breakfast by myself," I said with a proud smile.

"Yes, I can see that," he said as he looked around at the cleaned up area.

"I told you the other day that you would have to go back with Miriam tomorrow but now that Javier and Felicia have left, I was wondering if you wanted to stay until they return. I spoke with Jason and we decided that we can pay you cash if you want or maybe work out some other type of payment system. We are going to take a chance on you and your word that you are not a felon or wanted by the law. It is just so busy here now that neither Jason nor I have time to hire and orientate someone new. You know how things are run here now and we both know it is temporary, so if you can work a little longer until we actually have the time to find a replacement or until Javier and Felicia get back we all would appreciate it very much. It appears that you are a good hard worker and doing a fine job."

"Thank you Sheldon, I can do that and I appreciate the opportunity."

"Fine then," He tipped his cowboy hat at me and started to leave.

Before he got up from his chair, I thought this would be a good time to ask about a couple of ideas that I had, as I had nothing to lose at this point. "Sheldon, would you or Jason object if I made a new menu and a few changes here? Some of the ways that Javier did things were...well, I think he made more work for himself than he had to and I would like to streamline this kitchen work a little better than how he has been running it."

"It's all yours Missy. You're in charge of this kitchen now."

"Thanks, I appreciate your confidence in me!"

"You're welcome."

I went back to the kitchen with a piece of paper and a pencil and started writing down a new menu with an extended grocery list for Miriam as well as a some newly restructured processes for this kitchen.

I soon had my two weeks of food menu planned and a with a grocery list in hand for Miriam. Javier failed to tell me if I was to take the list up to Miriam or if I was to call her to come down and get it. I decided since I have not met her yet, that I should hand carry it up there and introduce myself. I was greeted by a tall blonde woman with ivory skin and fake looking boobs. "Great one of those types," I thought to myself…high school beauty queen gone pedestal trophy wife. There was a familiarity about her that I couldn't quite put my finger on but went on with my introductions.

"You must be Miriam?" I asked assuming it was her.

"Yes."

"Hi, I am Missy. I am replacing Javier and Felicia for the cooking and the laundry."

"Oh yes, yes Missy. Sheldon said he hired an extra person…and thank heavens he did. If he didn't, I would have to run that kitchen and right now there is no way I could find the time to do that besides all the office work and other responsibilities I have here. Just having two kids in activities keeps me hopping."

I smiled and nodded back at her acknowledging her busy life. "Have you heard anything from Javier or Felicia?" I asked.

"No, we haven't but I am sure they made it there by now and are with their son."

"That was very unfortunate for them. It didn't sound very good at all," I replied.

"Yes. Well come on in," she exclaimed showing she was nicer that my first impression of her.

I accepted her invitation and started to remove my shoes before entering the house.

"Oh my, leave your shoes on. We have kids running in and out of here like crazy. I don't even try to keep up with a dirty entry way," she giggled.

"Okay, thank you. Um, I have a grocery list for you. I wasn't sure if Javier brought it up here for you or if you come and get it or what, so I just brought it up here."

"Oh, that's just fine. Whatever is convenient for you," she smiled.

"If it is not too much trouble I was hoping that you could pick up a few personal items for me? Sheldon said he could pay me a wage in other ways, so I was hoping that you could take these expenses out of my first paycheck. I need a hair dryer, some crème rinse and some other personal items," and handed her a separate list for my personal needs.

"Of course Missy, no problem at all," she smiled. "Come on in and have some coffee with me. We can get to know each other."

She led me to the kitchen area where we sat down to drink our coffee. The house was beautifully decorated with a ranch style theme. She was correct in her earlier statement; the inside of the house looked like a lived in house. Not messy by any means, just not one of those model homes that you are afraid to sit anywhere. It was homey. We just started to drink our first cup of coffee when her two children opened the front door and started to run by us.

"Whoa, hold up there you two. I want you both to meet Missy. She is replacing Javier and Felicia in the kitchen. This is Jack and this beautiful young lady is Lindsay. Both kids stopped and gave me a ten second courtesy greeting before pushing each other and racing to the adjacent room together. It was a matter of seconds before Jack screamed.

"Mom! She stole my remote control to the X-Box and won't give it back!"

"I did not crybaby, I got it before you!"

"I called it first!"

"Did not!"

Miriam rolled her eyes at me, "School is not even out for the year. There was a half day today and they are already fighting. It's going to be a long summer."

I just smiled contently back at her appreciating the typical and normal family life. Her children's biggest worries in their innocent lives were who got control of the X-Box control. None of them had to worry about going to bed hungry or sleeping in abandoned buildings. They had the happy and content life that most everyone typically dreams of.

It was over an hour later when I finally thanked her for the coffee and excused myself to go back and start preparations for the evening meal. Walking back to the Lodge, I thought of how first impressions are so wrong. Miriam was beautiful; she had a beautiful house, a kindhearted husband and normal children. She seemed to have it all yet she was down to earth as the sky is blue. She was easy to get to know and easy to visit with. She portrayed someone who was content with who she is and the life she was living. It was nice. Nice to see someone who was good and normal; unlike the place I came from less than a week ago.

That night for supper, I made baked ham with whipped potatoes and white ham/milk gravy. I was going to make some beans as a side dish but thought they were probably all tired of beans, so I made some candied carrots instead along with some corn bread.

It appeared everyone was at their usual spots in the dining hall for supper but was unusually quiet as everyone seemed to be concentrating on eating the food that was placed before them. About half way through, I thought this was a good of time as any and decided to make my announcement.

"Can I have everyone's attention please? My name is Missy McDonalds and you have probably seen me around the last couple of days working with Javier. Sheldon or Jason may, or may not have informed you that Javier and his wife Felicia, who normally are the cooks here, had to go back to Mexico for a family emergency and will not be back for a while. Therefore, I will be taking over their duties. Since I will be doing all the cooking and laundry by myself, I have a few changes for you all to be aware of." I looked around the room and all had stopped eating and turned their attention to me.

"If you want clean towels, wash cloths and bed linens, we have a large supply in the laundry room, which is right over there next to the kitchen. I will not be entering your private cabins to strip your beds and gather the dirty towels or personal dirty clothes. You can bring your dirty clothes, linens and towels to the laundry room when you come for any of your meals and put them in the large gray laundry bins, which are located inside the laundry room. It is very simple; one says 'PERSONAL' for your clothing and other is labeled 'LINENS/TOWELS' for your dirty towels and your bed sheets."

"Secondly, as of tomorrow everyone gets a bagged lunch for your noon time meal regardless if you are around the ranch or not. You can eat it here in the dining area or wherever you want but there will no longer be a separate hot lunch prepared. When you are done with your breakfast, I will have all your lunches boxed up for you on the table next to that side wall," and pointed to the table next to the wall.

"Lastly, when you are done eating, please bring up your dirty dishes and throw any leftover food scraps into the garbage here." I pointed to the large garbage can in front of the dining tables and next to the kitchen counter. "Then you can take your plates and silverware and place it in this large gray bucket that I have sitting on the counter next to the garbage can," and then pointed to the gray tub so make it as clear and simple as I could get it.

"Thank you and I hope you all enjoy the food I will be preparing for you until Javier returns. Oh, one more thing. I will have dessert ready for you every night after supper and will leave it out until 8pm so that if you get a hankering for something sweet later in the evening, just come in and help yourselves. Tonight, I have carrot cake with cream cheese frosting. Desserts will always be on the same table where you will be picking up your lunches after breakfast."

I scanned the room and noted that everyone was just staring back at me unemotionally. A few nodded as if they understood the directions and then they all started to eat again without any rebuttal. I looked over at Jason, in hopes to get some type of reaction but he didn't seem to be any more bothered than anyone else. Surprisingly, with no complaints, I went about my chores in the kitchen while they finished their meal.

It was the tall quiet Native man who was one of the first ones to get up and bring his empty plate to the kitchen area. After he cleaned up his plate, he stood there as if he wanted to say something. There was a strange moment of silence before he finally spoke up.

"Ma'am?"

I smiled at his words and his shyness, "Please, call me Missy."

"Okay then, Missy. My name is Tommy Smith and I am the only person here who works all year around on the ranch." He hesitated again, "I just wanted to tell you that this was one of the finest meals that I have ate since...well, since...ever!"

"Thank you Tommy. I appreciate that," as I beamed with internal pride. "You will have to tell me some of your favorites and maybe I can make them up for you sometime."

He nodded in confirmation, "If all your meals are as good as this, anything you make will be fine." He then turned and again, re-rinsed his hands in the sink next to the door, put his cowboy hat back on and left without any dessert.

CHAPTER SEVEN

The next morning I had some left over oatmeal from the morning's breakfast meal. The left over oatmeal wasn't enough to save for the crew and I had already eaten so instead of just throwing it out, I thought maybe Molly would possibly eat the rest of it. I had watched Javier give her some table scraps from time to time and hopefully Molly would like the oatmeal as well as the guys did. If not, I'd just throw it out with the other garbage later.

Molly was waiting for me as I went outside to feed her. I poured the oatmeal in her bowl and topped it off with her dog food and then filled up her water bowl. I watched her as she lapped up the oatmeal like it was candy avoiding the dry food that was mixed in her bowl. I went back into the kitchen feeling quite smitten with myself that everyone was enjoying my new food choices, including the dog.

It was later that afternoon before I started getting things ready for the supper meal when I saw a black bag of trash that I had forgotten to take out earlier this morning. I carried it back outside and threw it in the dumpster but as I turned to go back into the kitchen, I saw Molly in her bed panting heavily in her little nook area where she sleeps. She didn't look well so I went over and gave her head a rub.

"What's the matter girl?" She just looked up at me with sad eyes as if she was in pain. I rubbed my hand over her back and her side when I realized her stomach was hard as a rock and there was blood was on her bed.

I pulled my hand back in horror. My God, the oatmeal I fed her at breakfast must have been bad for her. The first thought that came to my mind is that the oatmeal probably expanded in her stomach and now is having stomach cramps and bowel problems. All I could think of is that I have poisoned her and was probably responsible for her getting sick and in pain. I had to find Jason or Sheldon to help her. I took off running to the front of the building in hopes that one of them would be around to get Molly to the Veterinarian before she died. With a quick glance of the surrounding buildings and yard, I didn't see anyone in plain sight. They were like the police, always around until you need them and then they are nowhere in sight.

I jumped on the ATV that Felicia would drive to pick up the linens. I quickly figured out how to turn it on and stepped on the gas pedal. I sped out to the barn and unfortunately didn't find anyone inside of the first barn. I got back on the ATV and drove quickly to the other barn where I immediately saw Tommy trimming the hoofs of one of the horses.

"Tommy, Tommy," I yelled. "Come with me. Molly is sick. Come quickly," I screamed waving my arm in a coming motion.

Tommy obviously saw my despair, dropped the horse's hoof and tools and ran with me to the ATV. We both jumped in without buckling and we sped across the ranch as fast as the vehicle would go.

"I think I did it to her. I mean, I think I poisoned her. I gave her some oatmeal. I didn't realize that it probably expanded in her stomach. There was blood and she's in pain. Do you think her stomach or intestines will just burst?"

I could feel my eyes started to fill up with tears from the shame and guilt. "I didn't know dogs couldn't eat oatmeal. How was I supposed to know that? I never owned a dog before! What if she dies?" I exclaimed in panic fearing the worst, and even more horrid was how I would have to tell Jason and Sheldon and his kids that I killed their dog! Tommy just held on to the roll bar handles of the ATV. He was silent, per his usual demeanor; however, with my constant blubbering he was unable to get a word in edgewise.

We pulled up to the lean-to and ran up to Molly together. When we arrived and saw Molly, I gasped as to what I saw. I burst out crying from the pent up fear and anxiety. I turned to Tommy and buried my head into his chest and bawled like a baby. Tommy put his strong arms around me and started to laugh out loud.

"Well, Missy, I can assure you that you did not cause Molly's pain," as he rubbed my back to comfort me with his massive hands. I started to laugh with him as I pulled away and dried my eyes and nose with my shirt sleeve. I turned back to Molly as she was licking a little gray puppy that she just delivered.

Tommy and I watched and petted Molly as she delivered 3 more pups. I have never seen puppies being born before but was totally amazed at the whole ordeal. Neither Tommy, nor anyone else on the ranch knew she was pregnant. There aren't any other dogs around here, so who would have even guessed? Tommy stated that he thought she was just getting fat because Javier was feeding her too much. With her thick coat of fur covering her body, no one could visually see she was pregnant.

Tommy and I decided that we should name the first gray puppy "Oatmeal" considering he was gray and the circumstances to which he was born.

Tommy finally left to go back to work and I went back to the kitchen and called Jack and Lindsay, Sheldon and Miriam's kids, to come down to the lodge. I told them that I had a surprise for them. Once they got there I took them out back by Molly. This time I was on the receiving end of watching their eyes get three times bigger and mouths drop. They, unlike me, didn't cry like a big baby but they both squealed with joy at the new found puppies.

"Awesome! When did she have puppies?" Jack giddily asked.

"Just a little while ago so don't touch them yet. They are born with their eyes closed and cannot open them yet. Tommy told me they have to get used to their mom's smell the first couple of days. After that, we can play with them till our hearts content. But, I thought maybe you two would like to name them."

"This is sooo cool" cried Jack again.

"I should let you know that Tommy and I named that little gray one Oatmeal. She was the first one born. Because the fact that she is gray and I fed Molly Oatmeal this morning, we thought that name would be the most fitting," avoiding telling them the rest of the story.

Lindsay was less vocal than Jack but finally said, "I think since you named the first one Oatmeal, we should name the others after breakfast foods too. As a matter of fact, I think the one that has that horseshoe looking patch on its back should be named Lucky, as in 'Lucky Charms' cereal."

"Ya, and that one who is kicking its hind legs there; it should be called 'Kix'", said Jack.

We had a hard time coming up with the last one but agreed to try and keep the cereal theme going. For the last puppy, Jack came up with Fruit Loops but we decided that we didn't want it to grow up with a complex so we finally decided on 'Honey' which would be short for Honey Nut Cheerios. So there they were: Oatmeal, Lucky, Kix, and Honey. It was an exciting time and a precious bonding experience I had with the children.

As usual, Jason and the ranchers started to meander in for supper and immediately started eating when I noticed Tommy wasn't at his usual spot. Just as I was wondering why he wasn't there, he arrived and per usual performed his typical pre-meal routine. Since he was late, he ended up being one of the last ones to finish up. Instead of bringing his dirty dishes up, he got up from the table washed his hands and left his cowboy hat on the rung, then went outside the dining room doors. I wondered what in the world he was doing. It was so unlike him to just get up and leave, especially without his hat. Then, he came back in. He was carrying a handful of flowers in his hand as he walked up to me.

"It is hard to find flowers this time of the year, but I found a few wild flowers and Miriam had a few peonies that she said I could cut for you. I wanted to give these to you since you had a very emotional day. I was hoping these would make you feel better."

"Oh, they are beautiful and they smell wonderful. You are going to make me cry again. I am only on a 'once a day' cry regiment, are you trying to mess me up?"

"I am sorry, I will take them back then," he stated as he grabbed for the flowers in jest.

"Oh no you won't!" I retorted as I pulled the flowers back away from his reach. "Tommy, they are beautiful. I think that is the most thoughtful thing anyone has ever done for me." I gave him a big hug, "Thank you so much!"

"How is our patient doing this evening?" he asked.

"I am not sure. I haven't been out there in a while. Let's go see," I replied. "As long as we are going outside, how about giving me a hand with this garbage bag?"

"Sure." He grabbed the black garbage bag and frowned, "My goodness, this is heavy. Do you take this out every night?"

"Yep. Sometimes twice a day. Check out the gun show," I said as I put my arms over my head and flexed my biceps.

"I better watch out for you. You might just turn into a cowgirl if you keep this up."

I smiled and we walked out together. We saw that Molly hadn't moved from her spot that we earlier left her in. All of her puppies were curled up and sleeping close to her. I brought her water bowl over to her and she lapped it up as if she was dehydrated.

"Whoa, she was thirsty," said Tommy. "You are good with animals. I can see that."

"Who'd of thought, huh?"

He hesitated a moment..."Missy?"

"Ya."

"Would you like to go for a horse ride with me this Sunday? I think Jason would give me a few hours off…and if we have time we could also check out some cattle herds and make sure the ranch hands are doing their jobs. That way, I could show you the around the ranch and the land." He was shy and I could see that he was a little self conscious about his question.

"Really? I would love that. Sunday would be the best day since the ranchers help themselves to their supper meal. We have to go after the breakfast meal and after I get the food done for the supper meal. I can make a chili or something that is easy to heat up. Would two o'clock be okay? I can pack us a picnic supper for us, if that sounds good to you?"

"Great, sounds perfect."

"I have one problem though, I have never ridden a horse before, so you are going to have to show me how that is done. The thought of riding a horse is very intimidating but sounds exciting at the same time."

"If you can carry out these heavy bags of garbage twice a day, then you have the muscles to ride a horse. It'll be a piece of cake and speaking of cake, I am going to get one of your delicious pieces of cake and call it an evening. Let me walk you back inside."

CHAPTER EIGHT

Sunday afternoon Tommy and I walked to the back of the barn toward the last stall when we came upon a brown horse with a black mane. "This is Jenny. She is our oldest horse and we don't ride her much anymore. I am going to have you ride her. It is good to ride her once a week or so to loosen her joints a bit and keep her limber. She will be the tamest and an easy horse for you to ride." He gave her a double pat on the neck as I petted her soft nose a couple of times. He led her out of her stall and walked her over to the saddles.

"For now and in the future, I am going to have you saddle your own horse." He then proceeded to show me how it was done and when done, he took the saddle back off and made me saddle her myself. Even though I was nervous about saddling her, I thought that was very smart teaching tool.

Once I had saddled her to his satisfaction, he showed me how to get on and off the horse. After a few mounts off and on, he mounted the horse and sat behind me. He handed me the reins after showing me how to hold them. He then gave me a quick ten minute lesson on how to start, stop and turn her before he dismounted to let me practice for a little bit in the yard while he saddled his own horse. A few minutes later he was on his horse and we were soon riding side by side away from the small radius in which I have been living in the last week or so.

After riding for about fifteen or twenty minutes, a beautiful view came into my vision. It was like a picture out of a magazine. The horizon was full of hills and valleys and everything was green, luscious and bursting of life and beauty. The smell went from shrub weeds and animal smells to fresh greens and the floral of wild flowers. It was simply breathtaking. I stopped my horse and just took in the splendor around me.

"Wow, I never realized there was such beauty in the United States. I have lived a secluded life I guess," I stated in awe and wonderment.

"This is all I have known since I was a young. I cannot imagine living anywhere else. I would never change a thing," he replied.

"You grew up in this part of the world?" I asked as we continued riding along side by side.

"Yes. In a small town about twenty minutes from here. Jason and I were friends in school and in the summer, I would beg to come out to the ranch and help out. After I graduated from high school, they hired me on full time and I have been here ever since."

"I see," I said pondering about what my childhood may have been like. Suddenly a wave of sadness overcame me for not knowing. I knew when I was done at the ranch I was going to make a gallant effort in finding out who I am and where my home is at.

We trotted up a small hill and when we got to the top, I could see a big meadow below us with a big metal structure on it.

"What is that?" I asked curiously.

"It's an irrigation system for the field."

"Like a big water sprinkler?"

"Yep, just like a big water sprinkler," he said amused at my comparison. "We have quite a few of them on the property. Sometimes I think they are more work than benefit."

"Why? What do you mean?"

"As far as the land needing the water; it is a 'hit and miss'. The amount of water we need every summer depends on the amount of winter snow that falls here in the valleys and in the mountains. Every spring Jason and one of the hired men have to service every one of them. They have to verify if all the electrical connections are functioning, check the gear case levels, and make sure the nozzles are unplugged and free for water to flow through and things like that. It takes Jason and a hired man several days to service them up for the summer months."

"Wow that is a lot of work."

"Yes, there are a lot of things to do on a large ranch to support its operations. Many people do not understand or realize all the operational duties and responsibilities that we manage. Most people think we just cultivate the fields, harvest hay and feed the cattle, but there is so much more," he stated. "I could go on forever, but it would only bore you," he smiled.

We rode on for another thirty minutes or more until we came upon a small flowing river in the valley below us. "This is where we can water the horses and rest up for a few minutes," said Tommy.

"Sounds good. Are you getting hungry yet? If you are, we could eat here as well."

"That would be great. If you want to find a spot and get our food ready, I will take care of the horses and find some wood to make a small fire."

I started to lay out the blanket when I saw Tommy down by the river's edge washing up his hands. I looked down at my own hands, only to see that they were dirty also from the riding the horse and saddling her. Before going any further, I went to the river's edge next to Tommy and started to wash up as well.

"This river isn't very deep," I stated to make conversation.

"It's not a river," he replied. "It is a creek."

"A creek?"

"Yep. It is called 'Sucker Punch Creek'."

"That's a funny name," I replied with a contorted scowl.

"Do you know what a sucker fish is?" he asked.

"There is a fish that is called a sucker? I know the basic fish like walleye and trout and so forth but there is actually a fish called a sucker?"

"Oh yes," he exclaimed. "Suckers are very aggressive and that is how this creek got its name," he stated with a little drama in his voice, as if he was about to tell me a secret.

"So why do they call this Sucker Punch Creek? That doesn't make sense. If suckers are mean or bad, why wouldn't they have named it Bad Sucker Creek or something like that," not understanding how the two were related in any way.

"Well, I haven't gotten that far yet. Back in the day, a couple of young boys were playing by the river..."

"I thought you said this was a creek," I interrupted him.

"Um yes, the creek. Anyway, the boys were playing by this creek when one of the boys fell in. It was the spring time and the water was cold and the suckers were plentiful as it was spawning season. Fish swim upstream in the spring time to spawn," he said on a side note.

"The river was strong and the suckers were all around him like piranhas. The young boy was having a hard time making it back to the edge of the bank so the other little boy jumped in to help him. By the time the second little boy got into the water to rescue him, the current was already taking the first little boy down river. The second little boy just couldn't get to him."

"Oh my God, did he drown?" I asked with eyes wide open at the scary story.

"Well, the second little boy ran back to his home and got help. By the time the adults got back to the scene, they found the first little boy on the shore with round sucker marks all over his body. He was dead but they could see that he didn't drown."

"How'd he die?"

"Massive blood loss. All the blood was drained from his body; the suckers sucked all the blood out of him," he said very serious slightly moving his head back and forth.

"That is horrible. I mean, what a sad and horrible thing to happen," I said with utmost intrigue. I envisioned the scenario while taking a few steps back and away from the edge of the water.

I became confused again and said, "I still don't understand why they call this 'Sucker Punch Creek'? It falls back to my first comment...they should name it 'Blood Sucker Creek' or 'Bad Sucker Creek' but why 'Sucker Punch Creek'? I don't get it."

Before he responded he gave me a light punch on my right shoulder and said, "Sucker punch!"

"Ouch, why'd you do that," I retorted as I rubbed my shoulder where he punched it.

"Because you are a sucker for believing me; that was a made up story. Suckers really don't suck the blood out of people," he laughed at my gullibility. "The creek really doesn't have a name; it is just a small creek branching off the main river up north."

"Really? Why'd you tell me that then?"

"Well, now this is a true story. When Jason and I were young boys and would have friends out on the ranch, we would usually come out here to play, fish and build forts and stuff. For some reason, Jason and I would think it was funny to tell our friends crazy stories about the creek and if they believed us, we would sucker punch them as hard as we could on the shoulder. We would tease them and tell them they were suckers for believing the story. Each time Jason and I would come up with a different story for different friends. We'd feed off each other making the stories more believable," he smiled. "It was just one of the dumb boy pranks we did as kids," he said with a snort.

"That's horrible," as I smirked back at him.

"Just be thankful that I just gave you a little tap on the shoulder and not the real sucker punch we gave to our friends. They were black and blue for days."

"Whatever," I retorted and started to walk back to the area where the blanket was laid out.

Back at our blanket, I started to set up and prepare our supper meal, while Tommy built a small fire next to us. When the fire was started, Tommy sat down next to me on the blanket. He warmed and served up the chili while I prepared our bread and drinks. I was about to start eating when Tommy bowed his head and started to pray out loud.

"Father of the heavens and earth, we humbly thank you for the food that you have put before us. Thank you for the animals that you put on the earth and their sacrifices to give us nourishment. Bless those who are less fortunate than us and help nourish their body and souls. Amen."

I thought about Aunt Bev with the words in his prayer and how she provided me with food and water when I was so ill. I wondered if Tommy's earlier prayers went to God and then down to me. I had to think so. I don't think I could have survived any other way.

Again, I was in awe at Tommy's methodical and rhythmic traditions as well as his gratitude of thanks that he said in prayer. You wouldn't think this large and lean somber Native Indian man could be so sensitive. He was so much different than those I typically know. Hmmm, another memory. I must hang out with asshole men in my previous life, even though I don't know who they are.

I liked it here on the ranch and this beautiful spot but this moment again, made me more determined to find out where my home is, my roots and who I am; but there is nothing I can do about it right now.

"So, you and Jason have been friends since you were both young huh? That is a long time."

"Yes. He took me under his wing when I moved here."

"How old were you and where did you move from?" I asked for sake of conversation.

"I was nine when I moved to this area and off of the Reservation."

"So you are Native American then....I mean I thought you were but I guess I should never assume."

"Ute tribe."

I thought about that for a second and not being familiar with the Ute Indians nor any Native Indians as far as that is concerned. "You said your last name was 'Smith'. Is that a common last name of the Ute Indians?" I asked.

He started to chuckle a bit at my naivety and said, "No, Smith is definitely not a Native name. I was adopted by a white couple; John and Helen Smith. I was legally born Tommy Etsitty. My native name is Little Wing."

"Seriously? Indians really do give their children animal names like on the old western movies and stuff?"

"Yes, yes they do," he replied again giving me another little chuckle.

"Why do they do that?" I asked with curiosity?

"Well, first of all, the names are not always names in relation to animals; they are related to nature, whether it is earth, water, animal or whatever. Anyway, Ute Indians are known to always be in harmony with nature. We have a spiritual core and connection with our physical surroundings and resources the earth gives to us; past, present, and future. We believe nature lives in multiple dimensions."

"Interesting," I said before he went on to finish his explanation.

"When a child is born, the parents give the child a spiritual earthly name as to what is happening around at the time of birth. We believe that was brought to us from natures past. Parents give their children different names for each growth period in our lives. Since I was adopted later in life, I never got a 2nd or 3rd name. So, I will always go as Little Wing as my native name."

"Wow, that is so cool," I said in amazement.

"Seriously though, my native Grandma confessed to me that my native parents named me Little Wing because they were very into Jimmy Hendrix, the rock star from the 1970's and their favorite song was Little Wing, which Jimmy Hendrix created and sang. My native parents never did admit to it publicly to the native people anyway," he said snickering. "They were true hippies from the 60's and early 70's."

"Do your parents still live around here?" I asked.

"My adoptive Dad is in a nursing home and Mom died a long time ago. They were very old when they adopted me; I think in their late 50's."

"They gave me a good life. Dad was a very ethical man and was an accountant. Mom was very much into correct grammar, etiquette and manners and instilled those traits in me. She was a substitute English teacher and taught piano after school and on some Saturdays."

"If you don't mind me asking, why were you adopted? Were you taken away from your hippie parents?"

"No, my native parents both died in a car accident when I was little. They were high or drunk and driving somewhere. Long story short, they basically drove off a mountain cliff."

"Oh, no," I exclaimed. "I am so sorry Tommy."

"It's okay. I barely remember too much of them or much of the details when they died. I was only about five years old when they died." He hesitated for a moment before he began to speak again, "I was told that they left me home one night when they went out drinking. They never returned. I guess it was about a week before I finally walked over to one of the neighbor's home on the reservation and asked her if I could eat some of their food. I guess I must have been really hungry."

"I don't remember any of this really as I was so young. The only real things I do remember is wondering where my Mom was at and why she didn't come and feed me. I remember sleeping in their bed alone one night because they weren't there...but that is about it. Anyway, the neighbor knowing my parents had some issues, had her husband go over there only to find they weren't there."

"I am so sorry to hear that Tommy," I said sincerely. "So you were adopted after that?"

"No, after that, I went to my native Grandparent's place for a while before they both finally died. Grandma died shortly thereafter from diabetes and kidney failure and Grandpa died a few years later from aspiration pneumonia. I guess he was an alcoholic too and one of his drunken nights he inhaled a bunch of his vomit. He was in such poor health due to his alcoholism that he was not able to pull out of it. I was nine when he died. After that, I was put into the foster care system where I was adopted out by John and Helen Smith. It was my native grandfather who taught me and instilled the native ways and traditions in me and for that I am forever thankful."

"My Mom died when I was a little girl too," I said finding that we had a commonality. After I said that and before he had a chance to response, I got up from my sitting position and yelled, "I had a Mom who died of…of...of...breast cancer!" I started to laugh. "I remember. Yes, I remember her. She had brown hair like me. I remember her being sick and throwing up a lot and I had to bring her soup and water!"

By this time I was almost jumping up and down. I looked down at Tommy who was looking at me with a strange look on his face. Then it dawned on me that he didn't know why I was happy about knowing why my Mom died of breast cancer when I was just a little girl.

I sat back down on the blanket and took his hand. "Can I tell you something Tommy?"

"Sure."

I proceeded to tell him about my loss of memory and how I didn't remember anything about myself or my life prior to waking up next to the dumpster. "I know I must have been through a traumatic event but that's it, everything else was blank until then." I told him that every once in a while something comes back to me, as it did right now with my mother.

"It's always bits and pieces of something. Sometimes I have a 'Déjà Vu' type of thing when I smell something or someone says a word about something…like it is familiar to me yet I am just unable put my finger on it."

He didn't say and word, just smiled at me as if he was mesmerized by my story. As he was smiling, it was the first I time noticed his deep set dimples on each side of his cheeks. I was drawn to him. The way he was looking at me as if we were connecting telepathically without saying a word. I loved the way he spoke in a methodical and clean manner. His mannerisms were slow and steady. He appeared to be a stable and secure man, yet a little mysterious.

His eyes were deep set and were a deep chocolate brown; but those dimples....those dimples made my heart melt and suddenly my stomach was doing flip flops. I knew right then and there, at that moment, he was my soul mate. Our conversation just flowed back and forth and I felt like we clicked. I am not sure he was feeling the same way about me but I was hoping so.

"I need to go get something. I will be right back," he said as he put his cowboy hat back on and walked away towards his saddle.

When he left, I cleaned up our picnic area and threw the food scraps in the creek for the fish to eat and then took the paper products and put them in the small fire that Tommy earlier made.

It was a few minutes later when Tommy came back carrying a small leather bag with fringes on it. Tommy asked that we both sit back down on the blanket.

"May I perform a Native ritual on you?" he asked.

Not sure what he was getting at, I cautiously asked, "What do you mean?"

"My Ute people have a sacred cleansing and purifying tradition. It is done with Sage. It is to remove the negative energy from your body and soul and removes it to another space. I want to bring you back into balance and clean your body and mind of the impurities that are blocking your memory."

"It won't make me high like that Peyote...ya know, like what we see Native Indians smoke on the television will it?"

"No, it is sage and a natural herb. And you must be serious about this. It is not a joke or a false legend or tale."

I could see passion in his words and face. I felt disrespectful for trying to make light of his offering. "I am so sorry Tommy, I meant no disrespect. I would be honored for you to perform it for me."

He just nodded as he pulled out a plastic bag from his leather pouch. In the plastic bag he removed some grayish looking weeds that were bound in a large cigar shape, which I assumed was the sage. He took out a large sea shell, a bird feather and a lighter.

He lit the sage and after it got to a bright red state, he snubbed the fire out in the shell. The sage started to smoke from the remaining embers. As he was doing that he said, "The shell represents water; the unlit sage and ashes represent the earth. The lighting of the sage represents fire and the smoke represents air."

As the sage was still smoking he held it by the right side of my head next to my cheekbone. He took the feather and fanned the smoke so that it as it blew toward my right ear. Then he put the sage near the left side of my face and fanned the feather again making the smoke flow toward my left ear.

He chanted something that I didn't understand as he was fanning the smoke by around my face. Then without any further ado, he snubbed the smoldering sage out completely in his shell and packed everything back into this leather fringe bag.

"The left side of your head lifted much more smoke. It turned dark and more billowy, so I said a native prayer for your healing and memory."

"Thank you, Tommy. Really, I mean it. It means a lot to me."

"Tugrayahk."

"Huh?"

"That means 'Thank You' in Ute."

"Tugrayahk," I repeated his words.

"One word down, only a few more to go," he said with a smile.

"One thing at a time. Let me try and remember my past before I start learning another language to memorize."

"We should be getting back," he stated as he looked over the horizon. "The sun will be going down in a couple of hours."

I quickly packed up the blanket and we both mounted our horses again for our trek back to the ranch.

We were on our way back home and sunset was slowly starting to go down over the mountains. The sky turned a bright orange color with stripes of blue/green. I was quietly enjoying the scenery when I heard a bunch of howling sounds in the distance.

"What's that?" I exclaimed, suddenly frightened from the sharp and echoing noise.

I could see Tommy somberly look across the open plain towards the mountain before he said, "It's the music of the mountains."

"Sounds like a bunch of dogs howling to me," I replied.

He smiled at my innocence of the country noises. "It is coyotes."

"Why are they making that racket all of a sudden?"

"They made a kill. When they make a kill, they howl to tell the others in their pack to come and feed. That is one of the reasons we have to have extra ranch hands on. The cows are birthing now and the calves are perfect prey for the coyotes, mountain lions and on a rare occasion, bear. We need men on horses watching the herds to assure their safety this time of the year."

"Do they eat humans?" I asked rather nervously.

He turned and looked at me with a very serious and piercing look. "Only beautiful females; with brown hair and brown eyes," he replied and then grinned at me showing his dimples once again.

That was the first flirtatious words he said to me which confirmed to me that he had romantic feelings about me and that this was probably a real date other than a nice gesture for a new employee of the ranch. I guess this is how cowboys date when you don't have the city life and city activities around you.

"Tommy?"

"Um hmm?" he replied not looking at me.

"Is there really a fish called a sucker fish or is that made up too?"

He turned and looked at me just giving me that dimple smile but didn't respond. We rode silently side by side back to the ranch as the sun set over the horizon.

CHAPTER NINE

Two weeks or so had passed when Jason approached me after the supper meal. "Missy, do you have a second?" he asked.

"Sure, what's up?"

"Day after tomorrow will be the last day for about half of our extra ranch hands. We are going to take them back to the city as we don't have any more work for them."

Hearing those words made me nervous that my time was up as well and I that would be going back to the city to live on the streets again. I suddenly felt anxious and overwhelmed with sorrow knowing my time was up. I could feel my heart thumping harder as I awaited his words of termination.

"We really had a good crew this year, so I was thinking about having a little going away party here in the dining room around 7:30 or 8:00pm and was wondering if you could make up a cake or some kind of a dessert along with some type of munchies. My daughter came in last night for a couple of weeks so she, Miriam and kids will be here too. I am going to bring a little beer in for the guys but could you also make up some punch for the kids and those who don't drink beer?"

In surprise and shock I said, "Yes, Jason, of course. I would love to do that for you and the guys. I can set up the tables extra nice and have an adequate little spread of goodies."

He arose from his chair and said, "I will tell the guys then." He tipped his hat at me acknowledging his departure. Before he left, he turned and said, "Missy, you are doing a really good job here. I have overheard the ranch hands, more than once rant and rave about your cooking compared to Javier. Oh, and speaking of Javier, I haven't heard one word from him but between you and me, I wouldn't be disappointed if he never did come back," giving me a naughty little smirk. "I mean, I liked Javier and Felicia but you are doing the job of two people and the food as well as your work ethics is just extraordinary."

I felt myself flush a little but yet beamed with pride. "Thank you Jason, that means a lot to me and I would be honored to host a little going away party here. I will have everything ready by 7:30pm."

Everyone seemed to like the spread I prepared for them. Jason had set up his I-pad to some portable speakers for a little back ground party music. It wasn't too much later when Miriam and the kids came down to participate in the celebration. When the kids saw me, they immediately started to tell me about all the activities they've been up to the last week or so. Jason's daughter Savannah was here for a few weeks for a summer visitation and she joined the fun as well.

The evening was moving along very well. I leaned back on the kitchen counter and looking across the room, I saw Jason with one foot up on a chair. He was laughing and flaying his arms around as he was telling some wild stories to some of the guys. Another group of guys were chowing down on the food, while the kids brought the puppies inside and played with them. Laughter and love was all around me. It made me feel good. It made me feel like I was a part of a real family group. I didn't realize how much I yearned for moments like this.

It wasn't too long before a very bluesy version of "Sweet Home Chicago" came on the radio when Mark, one of the temporary ranch hands, stood up and announced loudly, "It's about time we hear some soul music in this hick country ranch." The real cowboys started to boo him in jest as a couple of others clapped to support him. Mark was tall and lanky and swaggered as he walked as if he was a coolest dude around. He was starting to go gray and sported a gray goatee. He looked like he just stepped out of a Jazz band from Chicago or New Orleans. His looks reminded me of the movie actor Morgan Freeman. He always had a smile on his face and a story to tell and was always the life of every supper meal. Before I knew it, he pulled me from the kitchen counter that I was leaning on and started to twirl me around as we danced to the blues music. It wasn't before too long when Sheldon took Miriam and joined us in a dance. Jason decided to dance with his daughter as Tommy danced with Lindsay, Sheldon and Miriam's daughter.

Everyone hooted and clapped when the next song came on. It was the country song: "Momma Don't Let Your Babies Grow up to be Cowboys". Mark started to shake his head. Before leaving me on the dance floor alone, he bent over and kissed the back side of my hand and said, "Thank you for the dance my sweet lady."

Before I had a chance to thank him back, Tommy walked over to me, took my hand and started to waltz me around the floor. I was surprised at myself as I followed him pretty well. I laughed when I made a few mistakes but Tommy knew how to dance and led me around the floor with ease.

I went back to the kitchen area to grab a glass of ice water when Jason started chanting: "Tommy. Tommy. Tommy." Before long Sheldon, Miriam and the kids joined in the chant while rhythmically clapping their hands. I noticed a couple of ranch hands were also doing the same. I had no idea what in the world they were doing or why they were chanting Tommy's name. Could it be his birthday or something?

I looked at Tommy who was smiling before he finally yelled out: "Okay, Okay. But just one."

He walked to the back side of the dining room where a bed sheet was covering, what I thought was, some boxes of supplies or some ranch supplies of some kind. I never bothered to investigate what was underneath the sheets. When Tommy pulled off the sheet, he revealed an old brown upright piano. He pulled out the piano bench and sat down facing away from the crowd. He brushed his long hair away from his face so that it hung over and covered his back. Then he started to play.

He started with "Somewhere Over the Rainbow" and then without pause went into a Mozart or Beethoven classical piece. Not familiar with classical music I couldn't say what it was other than it was beautiful. I watched him as he passionately played. His fingers magically danced across the keys as his head moved back and forth following his fingers. I was jaw dropped and dumbfounded at his talent and gracefulness. I looked around the room and everyone else had the same expressions. The exception to the rest was Jason, Sheldon, Miriam and the kids who obviously had heard him play before. They all had big smiles on their faces; proud of their number one man.

Tommy finished up his piano piece with chopsticks as if his playing was no big deal. He stood up and turned to us and everyone whistled and clapped. Tommy walked towards me with a smirk on his face.

"After that, I think I'll grab a beer. I am a little rusty, it's been awhile."

"Are you kidding me Tommy? That was something out of this world. Who would have ever thought you could not only play piano, but play like some type of professional concert pianist," I declared loudly.

"You must have forgotten that my mother was a piano teacher. Since she was the teacher, there was no way I could give excuses not to practice. She couldn't have her own son be a slacker compared to her other students," he stated.

"Now that you are older and so talented, I suppose you are glad your mom pushed you."

"I hated the lessons and the practicing as a young kid because I wanted to go outside and play with my friends after school. So when I knew there was no getting out of them, I decided to practice every morning before school and that way I could still be with my friends. After a while, I got better and better and started to play every evening before going to bed. As I grew into an adult, it became therapeutic in a way. When it is not so busy around here, I will come in here and play. It gives me happy thoughts of my parents and my childhood."

While Tommy and I were talking, some of the ranch hands were leaving and a couple of them came up to me to say goodbye and to thank me for my wonderful meals. It was 10pm before the beer was gone and the left over ranch hands went back to their bunk houses. The kids left to go to Jason's house to play video games and Jason went with them stating he had to get up early to take the guys back to the city. This left Sheldon, Miriam, Tommy and I to clean up the mess. After everything was cleaned up, we sat around drinking coffee and talking close to midnight. We laughed and enjoyed the togetherness as I listened to them tell stories of the past ranch hands and the experiences they had with them. I was in the moment.

I went to bed that night feeling and thinking that I belonged here. Feeling and thinking that I no longer wanted to find out who I am. This is where I want to be.

CHAPTER TEN

The following week, life at the ranch was easier after half of the hired help was returned to the city. The amount of food I made was much less; the time it took to make meals was much less and the clean up was a snap. I wonder how much longer Jason and Sheldon will let me stay here as I hardly feel like I am pulling my work load. It was 3pm and supper was already prepared and ready to go. It was just a matter of warming it up prior to the supper hour.

Realizing I had a few hours to kill, I stepped outside to see what was going on around me. The sun was bright without a cloud in the sky. I let the sun rays warm me as I stretched my arms over my head and took a deep breath. The ranch smelled like a ranch but at the same time, the air was crisp and light and nothing like the air within the city. Breathing in this fresh mountain air felt as if a piece of heaven was filtering through my lungs and wrapping its sun rays around me giving me a big old hug of warmth and sunshine.

I stretched my torso from side to side. When I turned to the right, I saw Molly had brought the puppies to the front side of the building instead of the rear. The puppies were starting to learn how to play as they were nipping at each other's ears and lifting their tiny paws to bat at each other while Molly laid there keeping an eye on them They were just learning the beginnings of socialization. They were so innocent and carefree. Their cuteness made me smile.

No sooner was I smiling when I suddenly felt mixed with emotions once again. A yearning came over me. I thought about the fun bonding time with everyone we had last week at the going away party and coming to the ideation that this is where I want to be forever but seeing Molly's pups and reflecting back on Tommy's unusual childhood, I wondered what my childhood was like. I know I had brothers and a mom who had died when I was young, but was my life happy carefree and innocent like the puppies or was it abusive and horrible? Did I have a dad? Did I grow up in foster care? If not, where is my family? Am I married? Then the most horrid thought came to me which I have never thought of before. It made me wonder if I had children of my own. Were they crying and wanting their mommy? Was I missing out on their young childhood...or worse yet, were they missing their mommy?

Is anyone out there looking for me...but if they were, why haven't they found me? With those thoughts, it made me rethink how long I have been missing. Was it longer than the time frame of waking up at the dumpster? Have I been going through life with some sort of memory loss for years and years?

All these questions really came to surface for the first time. I mean, I thought about things here and there but this was the first time that I really felt a passion and a real yearning to find out who I am and where I came from, even if it was a life that I wasn't proud of such as Sunny's. I needed to find closure before I could move forward.

I felt enlightened and overwhelmed with burden at the same time with all of these feelings coming to surface. I started to wonder where I would even start. Do I call 911? I knew calling 911 would be absurd but seriously...it made me really contemplating as to where and what would be my first steps.

I remembered Tommy telling me on our horse ride that when things get overwhelming and frustrating for him, he just saddles up his horse and goes for a ride in the mountains. He calls to the earth, the wind and the water while on the mountain edge. The spirit of the mountains clears his mind and soul and he becomes whole again.

I looked over at Molly and the puppies again. Oatmeal, the biggest of the bunch now was laying flat on his back napping next to his mother. With over two hours before supper, I walked out to the barn to ask Tommy if I could take a horse ride out on my own. Maybe the spirit of the mountains could ease my burdened mind.

I looked around both barns and no one was in sight. I went over to Jenny, the horse I rode the other day. I gave her a handful of oats and asked her if she would let me ride her (not thinking that I would actually try riding her without Tommy or someone to assist me). When I asked her if I could ride her, bizarrely she whinnied and shook her head up and down as if she was actually answering "yes" to my question. A little surprised and freaked out about a horse possible answering me, I felt like it was some strange sign that I could probably do this on my own. I know how to saddle her; I know how to brush her when I am done; I knew the trail that Tommy and I went on before, so why not? I wouldn't dare go as far as Tommy and

I had gone but the thought of a short independent ride made me start to get excited. I knew I could do this on my own and I wanted to experience that spirit of the mountains that Tommy spoke of so passionately.

I saddled up the horse without any problem what-so-ever and led her out of the barn and into the main yard area before I mounted her. Easy smeasy, I whispered to myself. It felt good. I was high above the ground. I felt in control and powerful as I steered the horse around the yard. For the first time that I can remember, I felt in charge of my destiny.

I trotted her out towards the hillside away from the ranch buildings knowing I had to be back within an hour or so to get cleaned up and get supper ready. We trotted a while before I became brave enough and go into a full gallop. It wasn't long before I reached the top of the large hill and stopped the horse. I looked around at the beautiful green hills and the mountains in the distance. My cheeks were cold from the wind upon my face from the fast gallop of the horse. This feeling that I had right now...at this moment...it was exuberance, freedom and purity. I wanted to scream at the top of my lungs. It was the spirit of the mountains making me whole again.

I sat there for a few minutes and took it all in before deciding to return to the ranch. I was proud that I could do this on my own. Proud of my accomplishments at the ranch and now felt strong and ready to take on the research and investigation of who I am.

The horse and I were almost back to the main yard of the ranch when the horse, without prompting, stopped in its tracks. She was hesitant to move forward and snorted, shook her head a bit and started to move backwards a couple of steps. I didn't know what was wrong with her as she wasn't acting normal. We were so close to home so I knew there weren't coyotes or wolves around to spook her but she was obviously spooked over something. I gave her a little kick and shook her reins to move forward. She still didn't move so I kicked her a little harder; shook the reins a little harder and yelled "hee-haw". What happened next all went in slow motion.

The horse reared itself up and as she did, I heard the sound that she must have heard that originally spooked her. It was a rattlesnake. She started to hoof the snake and I think she was trying to kick it with her hind legs too. I heard myself scream and I think scared the horse even more. I was no longer able to hold on to the horse any longer and fell onto the ground. I saw the horse take off running and the next thing I saw was Tommy was standing over me.

"Don't worry Missy, the ambulance is coming," I heard Tommy say in a concerned way.

I started to sit up. "What? What are you talking about," I stated dazed and somewhat disorientated.

"Lay back down now. You don't want to get up. Are you hurting anywhere?" Tommy asked.

"No, not really," starting to sit up again. This time Tommy allowed me to sit up. Now remembering that I fell from the horse, I wanted to explain why I was laying on the ground.

"I fell off the horse," I stated shaking my head back and forth as I rolled my eyes in embarrassment.

"The horse saw a rattlesnake and reared up and I fell off."

"A rattlesnake? Hmm, rattlers are pretty rare for this far north east but it was most likely a Midget Faded Rattler. It must have come out of the grassy area to sun itself."

I looked at him as if he was talking in some foreign language. "Aren't all rattlesnakes the same?" Before he had a chance to answer I continued talking, "Never mind, it doesn't really matter, all snakes are scary to me." As I was talking I felt the warm ooze of blood trickle down my face. I put my hand up to my forehead and Tommy stopped me.

"You have a bad gash over your forehead on your hairline. It's pretty deep. Are you sure you don't hurt anywhere?"

"Well, now that you mention it, ya I guess my forehead does kind of hurt a bit." Out of nowhere, I heard sirens of an ambulance coming towards our direction.

Before he had a chance to even respond the ambulance came into my view. "Oh seriously, you didn't" I whined. "I don't need an ambulance for crying out loud, Tommy, I am just fine," I moaned again feeling rather sheepish at the whole ordeal.

Sheldon's white diesel truck drove up with the ambulance right behind him. He got out of the truck and led the ambulance workers to where I was sitting.

"Well, it's here now," said Tommy. "You must have got knocked out for a couple of seconds or minutes and you're going to need some stitches on that cut, so you may as well go with them."

Before I had a chance to respond, the paramedics were there asking me questions and briefly checking me over and wrapping my head. They asked me if I could stand and, of course, I stood up without any problem.

"Yes, yes, I am fine," and walked towards the back of the ambulance with a paramedic holding on to my right arm. I knew better than to rebel any longer on taking an ambulance ride to the hospital, as I knew I would get defeated by everyone around me.

Before getting into the back ambulance, Tommy grabbed my arm and turned me towards him. "I will go with you to the hospital. I will follow the ambulance in the truck." Tommy then took me in his arms and gave me a big hug. "I was so worried! I am so glad you are okay."

I didn't have a chance to reply as the paramedics shuffled me in back of the ambulance and we drove off.

CHAPTER ELEVEN

The emergency room was like any other. My emergency room door was open and I could see people scurrying by pushing patients in carts or wheelchairs. There were beeps from various I.V.'s and in the far off I could hear a baby cry. There was an older man to the room left of me who must have had a stroke. I could overhear his wife and I assume his daughter, asking all sorts of questions of the physician. In the room to right of me, I believe there was a patient who was severely intoxicated. He must of been quietly sleeping or passed out because there wasn't a sound from the room but outside of his room there was a police man. I overheard the policeman tell the physician he was going to take him to detox once he was medically cleared.

My nurse was Judy and the physician who saw me was Dr. Martin. Dr. Martin performed a brief neurological and limited physical examination and then stitched up the gash on my upper forehead.

"Since the laceration is right on your hairline, it will hardly be noticeable," he exclaimed. "Just put some antibiotic ointment on it a couple times a day. The stitches can come out in five days. If it looks clean and not infected, you could have a nurse or physician assistant who is more local to you remove them. There is no sense in driving all the way back here just to remove a few stitches."

Since I was apparently knocked out and had a pretty good gash on my head, Dr. Martin also wanted to send me for some head X-rays and if results were okay, he would discharge me back to the ranch. I thought it was unnecessary and assured him I was just fine still feeling foolish about even being in this situation. Tommy insisted I follow the physician's advice and knowing I would lose that battle again with them both, I finally gave in.

"Okay, Okay, you guys win!" I yelled with a smirk. "But won't you both be embarrassed when you see the x-rays come up empty…supporting that fact that I have no brain!"

"Well, she didn't lose her sense of humor," Tommy responded in jest.

Finally, after about an hour waiting for my x-rays and some other type of scan they did, Dr. Martin briefly came in and told me there was a mild abnormality in my x-rays and he was going to have a neurosurgeon come in and see me.

"What is it?" I stated in surprise.

"I will let the neurosurgeon explain it all. He will be here shortly."

Dr. Martin barely got those words out of his mouth before he turned and left as if he was purposely avoiding any further conversation regarding the abnormal x-rays. I looked over at Tommy.

His lips were tightened and his nostrils flared. He gave me an 'I told you so' look.

"I wonder if I cracked my skull or if I am bleeding under my skull from the fall off the horse. Why else would a neurosurgeon need to see me? My head really doesn't hurt that bad. Well, it hurts like a bruise on my forehead area but I don't feel any head pressure as if my head in going to explode or something like that, and mentally I feel fine." I said to Tommy perplexed.

Tommy's expression went from 'I told you so' to sharing my concern. He took my hand and gave it a squeeze. "I will always be here for you," he said smiling at me as he brushed my cheek with his other free hand.

My heart was melting that someone cared about me. It sent tingles down my spine and once again, I saw those big dimples highlighting his perfect smile.

It was only a matter of minutes before a big African American man with a white physician's coat came in and shut the door behind him. "Hello Missy, I am Dr. Anderson," he said in a big booming voice. "I am one of the neurosurgeons on call here today and was asked to see you by Dr. Martin. I assume you were told that I was coming down to see you?"

"Yes, he did. He said there was some kind of abnormality in my head x-ray?"

"That's correct. I reviewed your x-ray and CAT scan with the reading radiologist and we both concurred that it appears you have a large piece of, what looks like, a bullet shrapnel lodged in the left side of your skull. That is why after your head x-ray, they sent you straight over to get that CAT scan."

I could feel my eyes widen as I dropped my mouth in shock. I looked over at Tommy who was doing the same. "Okay?" I said in the form of a question, not really knowing what else to say.

"Do you want to tell me what happened and when this occurred?" Dr. Anderson asked.

"What do you mean? I don't know when or what happened. I don't remember."

"It says here that you fell off a horse today which brought you in here but it is clear from Dr. Martin's report, that an external wound on the left side of your head has been healed for some time now…at least a couple of weeks or as long as a couple of months or so?"

"I am sorry, can you back up again," I said confused and still trying to absorb that news. "Are you telling me that I was shot in the head about month ago?"

"Yes, I am telling you exactly that."

A few moments passed as I was still processing the information. I was trying to figure out when or how I was shot; only to realize I didn't remember anything prior to waking up next to that dumpster in the city. "Dr. Anderson? Could a gunshot possible cause a memory loss?" I asked.

"A gunshot to your head? Yes, it most likely could," he nodded in confirmation. "Any major trauma to the brain could cause that. Are you having some memory loss?"

"Well, you are the first...well, second person I have told this to," looking over at Tommy before turning my attention back to Dr. Anderson. "It was about four or maybe five weeks now, where I just woke up one morning by a dumpster with a severe headache. I didn't know who I was, where I was, or what I was doing. The first week or so was just kind of a blur and I wasn't feeling well at all. I was going to...ya know, go to the police or something to get some help but long story short, I ended up working at the Parker ranch to temporarily cook for their ranch hands. Time slipped by so fast and my employment there was supposed to be very short lived so I thought I would get some help after I finished up there."

I looked over at Tommy and then looked down at my lap. I nervously started to twist my hair around my fingers, apprehensive to what I was about to say. "Besides getting shot, I…I think I was raped too. When I woke up, my crotch was a little bloody and it was pretty bruised up." I looked back up at Tommy in shame and as I did, I saw his eyes had started to well up with tears and his bottom lip tightened in anger. When Tommy saw me look at him, he quickly looked away so that I couldn't see him being distraught.

"Well that puts another twist on things," said Dr. Anderson. "Were you drugged?"

"That's just it. I don't remember. I cannot tell you."

Dr. Anderson sat back in his chair. I could see his mind thinking as he clicked his pen on and off several times.

"Okay. We are going to have to get a police detective in here because by law, we have to report any form of physical or sexual abuse and I will ask Dr. Martin to obtain some STD testing on you as well."

"STD"?

"Sexual Transmitted Diseases."

I didn't respond but nodded my head up and down to show understanding and agreement.

"The detective will need to come in to take your statement in regards to any crime. However, medically in regards to your memory problems and that shrapnel in your skull, I need to have you answer a few questions as best as you can in order to help me understand what exactly happened to you so that we can explore the best treatment options for you."

I then proceeded to tell him all that I could recall from the dumpster until now and how a few things are coming back to me like the fact that I was a career person, that my mother had died of breast cancer and that I have more than one brother. He occasionally interjected with a few questions and intermittently wrote a few things down on his clip board as I told him my story.

"Interesting," he stated. "From hearing your story, you obviously are suffering from a very severe case of amnesia. There are many forms or types of amnesia but what I believe you have is what we call 'retrograde' amnesia which statistically, is not very common. However, with that said, I have seen this twice before; once in my residency and again a couple of years ago when a patient came in with a severe brain trauma from a motorcycle accident. With retrograde amnesia, the patient cannot recall things from their past; however, is able to remember short term things such as what you ate for lunch, for example."

"I am fairly confident that this was caused from the gunshot wound to your head," he continued on. "You had stated that you believed that you were raped and with any severe traumatic event, can cause a psychogenic amnesia. Psychogenic amnesia is statistically limited to a memory surrounding that particular event and not your entire past, such as what you are experiencing. Some medications, such as Rohypnal, the date-rape drug, can also cause an anterograde amnesia, which means they don't remember anything they experienced while having that drug in their system…hence why they call it the date rape drug."

I nodded again showing him that I was able to understand his medical terminology before he began again.

He then stood up, grabbed the x-rays and put them on the light box for me to see. "As you can see here is the piece of bullet shrapnel lodged in your skull," as he pointed to a bright spot on the x-ray. "The bullet entered here above your left ear and most likely exited back out here, right behind your left temple leaving the majority of the bullet fragment right here next to the exit wound. This injury was isolated to only the left side of your skull and it doesn't appear that the bullet went into or damaged any of the brain tissue at all but if it did, it must have barely scraped it. Luckily for you, the person who shot you was not a very good shot."

"So if it only went into my skull and didn't do any damage to my brain, why do I have the amnesia?" I questioned. I looked over at Tommy who was also nodding inquisitively.

"That is a very good question," stated Dr. Anderson. "Secondary damage to the hippocampus, which is this part of your brain (he pointed to an area in the x-ray) occurred from the shock wave from the gunshot impaction. The hippocampus is the part of the brain that is associated with mainly long-term memory. Since there wasn't 'structural' damage to that area, I am fairly confident that over time, you will get your memory back and that area of your brain will recalibrate itself."

"I am a hunter myself and I have shot deer and other large game before, so why didn't the bullet cause more damage than it did?" asked Tommy who now seemed to be intrigued in this whole medical explanation.

"Another great question," replied Dr. Anderson. "The type and velocity of the bullet, as well as the type and caliber of the gun, are all variables that can make huge differences in the amount of damage that can be done. I think we can be fairly certain that this came from a handgun as handguns have slower moving bullets than higher level weapons, such as what the military use, like an AK-47 for example."

This time Tommy was nodding in understanding and assurance as this time the physician was talking more of his language.

"So, what to do from here," Dr. Anderson said as statement rather than a question. "As I mentioned already, we'll notify the local police department to have a detective come and see you. Dr. Martin will do some more tests on you to rule out any sexually transmitted disease that may have occurred from being raped."

"Neurologically, the bullet piece appears to be solidly lodged. The skull is very thick and hard and not a movable bone, such as your jaw or a joint, so it dislodging or moving is not likely. As long as it's not bothering you, I think it would be best to just leave it alone. If we take it out, there is always the possibility of doing more damage than if we were to leave it. With any surgery, there are always possibilities of complications such as infections and other issues. If you feel uncomfortable with that plan we could always take another film in a few weeks for a comparison, just to confirm its stability."

"No, actually I think I am okay with just leaving it where it is. I didn't even know it was there till now, so obviously it is not bothering me whatsoever."

"It's apparent your memory is slowing coming back...well at least memories of your past. You may never get the memory of the traumatic event of the rape or shooting, especially if you were drugged with Rohypnal. I would recommend seeing a therapist or even a neuropsychologist to help you digest this entire life changing event that has happened to you. They can also work with you on cognizance recollections to help you to regain some of those past memories of yours. I would like to see you in about a month. We can touch base again to see if you are having any delayed or systemic neurological problems. How does that sound?" he said with a smile.

"It sounds okay. Thank you."

Tommy stood up and shook Dr. Anderson's hand and also thanked him as a real gentleman would, again making an exemplary impression upon me with his character and manners.

CHAPTER TWELVE

Twenty minutes later, there was a knock on my door. A man in a black suit, white shirt and a striped tie walked in to my room, "Missy McDonalds?"

Tommy and I both turned and looked at him simultaneously. He had a presence which commanded our attention. The tone of his voice was strong and his speech was straight forward and to the point as he took charge of the room.

"Yes?"

"Hi Missy," he stated as he walked towards me to shake my hand. "I am Detective Simeon Gibson from the Investigation Bureau of the Salt Lake City Police Department. Dr. Anderson reported a possible rape and attempted murder. Do you feel up to talking right now and giving me a statement?" he asked.

Murder. The word sounded so strange that I was involved with anything of that magnitude. Murder, rape, kidnapping, gang wars, those types of things only happen in the movies.

"Sure, no time like the present," I said shrugging my shoulders.

He turned to Tommy and asked him to leave. Tommy was hesitant but I assured him that I would be okay alone with the detective. Once Tommy had closed the door to my room he took a chair next to my bed.

"Since we are not at the station house, this interview will be recorded. Do you have any objections to that?"

"No, that's fine, but I don't know what I can tell you as I don't remember too much."

"Well, let's just start with the first thing you do remember."

I repeated my story as I told it to the doctors however Detective Gibson asked quite a few more questions outside the medical realm. Other than the obvious, he asked a plethora of additional questions that had nothing to do with the rape and attempted murder. Questions such as: Who Tommy was and why was he here? When did I meet him? Where was I staying and why was I staying there? What are my bosses' names at the ranch and how can he get a hold of them? I understood that he was asking me all these questions to get a complete picture and timeline of how I ended up here, but it almost made me feel as if I was the bad guy and not the victim. It made me wonder since I really don't remember much of anything, maybe I was a criminal in my past life and his next question confirmed it.

"Would you be willing to come down to the station and give us your fingerprints?"

"Sure, I don't have anything to hide. I guess if I did something criminal in the past then I should own up to it, even though I don't feel like I was one." I said later as a side note, "I would even take a lie detector test if you want."

"No, I believe you Missy. The reason that I would obtain your fingerprints is because there are people who get fingerprinted in this world other than criminals," he said smiling at my response.

"All law enforcement, military, and some other government workers have to be fingerprinted. When we obtain your fingerprints, we can process them to see if they come up in any of our fingerprints data bases...good or bad," he said trying to ease my fear.

"Do you have any other questions or concerns for me?" he asked. When I did not, he shut off the recording device, gathered his papers and stood up.

"Thank you Missy. Obviously, with your lack of remembering anything prior to waking up by the dumpster, we don't have a lot to go on but I we'll see what I can dig up. Whenever you can get down to the station to get fingerprinted is fine but probably sooner than later or as soon as you feel up to it."

He handed me his detective card and wrote a case number on the back. "When you go in there, give them this case number and they will take it from there."

"Thank you, I will," I replied as I took the card. "We can go down there as soon as Dr. Martin discharges me from here."

"Good, good. Can I get a hold of you at the number you provided at the ranch?"

"Yes, please do."

He shook my hand again before leaving me alone in my hospital bed.

CHAPTER THIRTEEN

A week later and back at the ranch, I was finishing up with the supper dishes when Tommy walked into the kitchen area followed by Detective Gibson and a familiar man holding a bouquet of pink carnations. "Hey, Cassie," said the man.

Cassie, why did he just call me Cassie? And that voice; I know that voice. I stared at him knowing that I knew him from somewhere. Why does he look familiar? Then it hit me.

"J.D.! Oh my God. J.D.!" I screamed.

I could feel my lower lip start to quiver as I felt my heart beat faster. "J.D. I remember you." I just stood there as he walked up to me and handed me the flowers. I started to shake; it was my brother J.D.! It was not only seeing him again after all of this time but to know that I remember him and that I was getting my memory back. He slowly put his hands on my shoulders, lowered his head to my level and locked his eyes upon me. His eyes said, "It's ok now." I laid my head on his shoulder. All the hell, pain, strangeness that had happened to me in the last couple of months came spewing out in uncontrollable tears as I sobbed with raw emotion.

After a few minutes, he pulled me away. "Cassie, we have been so worried about you. I cannot believe we finally found you!"

"Have you been looking for me?" I asked between my sobs.

"Cassie! Yes! Yes, of course we have been looking for you," he replied in disbelief that I would even ask that question.

"Why? I mean we hardly ever talk to each other; why were you looking for me now verses any other time?"

"I tried to call you several times as I was coming up to Minnesota to go back to school for Chemical Dependency Counseling. I was hoping to stay with you until I got set up with my own place. When you never answered your calls, I tried to Facebook you but you didn't answer those either. I thought maybe you were angry with me so I had Jordan try to reach you but you didn't answer him either. That is when we all started to get a little concerned."

"You had listed where you worked on your Facebook page and I was able to talk to your boss. Your boss informed me that she made you take a month off but you were supposed to be back at work a couple of weeks ago and never returned. She had been trying to reach you also without success and was afraid that you were probably extremely upset with her, your job with her and the company.

After speaking with your boss, Jordan, Joseph and I were afraid that you had gone into a deep depression or worse case scenario, may have harmed yourself. We all agreed that I was the most available to go check up on you and since my plans were to go to Minnesota anyway, I took the first flight I could get. I went straight to your townhouse."

"When I got there, your door was locked so I called the police to come over and perform a welfare check on you. When the police opened the door, they saw weeks of your mail lying on the floor from your mail slot. They looked around and you were not there. That is when I went with the police back to the station and filed an official missing persons report."

"The detective in Minnesota that was assigned to the case tracked you down to your flight to Sacramento. Your white Lexus was still at the airport parking lot. They did some more investigating and found that your flight to Sacramento had an emergency landing here in Salt Lake City. Plane records confirmed that you never got back on the plane to Sacramento, so he contacted the Salt Lake City police department.

It was Detective Gibson, here in Salt Lake City who connected the dots," he said turning and smiling at Detective Gibson. He saw the missing photo that the Minnesota police provided for the Salt Lake police department and determined that you, Cassie, were the same person as Missy McDonalds. He immediately contacted the Minnesota detective who, in turn, contacted me and well, long story short, here I am."

Still dumbfounded and in disbelief, I stared at him as my thoughts and memories just started spewing out of my mouth. "Jordan and Joseph are our brothers; they're twins...and our last name is Miller. My director's name at work is....is...Lois; and she has red hair. I remember. Things are coming back to me now," I screamed in delight.

In the background I could see Detective Gibson and Tommy over J.D.'s shoulder, both standing there silently. Detective Gibson with his legs apart and arms crossed, while Tommy was holding his cowboy hat in his hand; both watching our touching bonding scene of brother and sister reuniting. I let go of J.D. and ran over to them.

Before I had a chance to say anything else, Detective Gibson said, "Cassie, can you verify this is your brother then?"

"Yes, of course!" I nodded with excitement.

"I will get back to the city then. In the next day or so, I will need you to come to the department to sign a few papers and close up the case. Do you still have my card with my number on it?"

"Yes. Thank you, Detective. I will come by tomorrow," and shook his hand in appreciation. J.D. and Tommy followed my lead, also shaking his hand before he turned and left leaving the three of us alone.

"Tommy, this is my brother J.D." I said with pride. "Come and meet him." I was almost jumping with excitement as I grabbed his hand to bring him closer to J.D. As I did, I saw that stoic demeanor in Tommy's face and mannerisms.

"Yes, Missy we already met and made our introductions outside. I was the one that greeted him and Detective Gibson when they pulled up to the ranch before bringing him in here to see you," he stated forcing a fake smile, trying to hide his sadness.

It then dawned on me that he was sad as I would be leaving. I would no longer be cooking for them and would be leaving the ranch; leaving Sheldon, and Miriam, Jason, and the kids. But mostly, I would be leaving him. I stepped back and looked back at him, realizing the same thing. My happiness fell back to a plethora of mixed emotions about the uncertainty of leaving here and what my future was going to hold. I turned and looked back at J.D. who by now could see the pain and uneasiness in our faces. He knew there was something there between us.

No words were spoken in those last few minutes, but all three of us felt that bond and understood the mixed emotions that were overpowering that happy moment. It was dead silence.

Finally Tommy spoke up, "Now that you have found your sister, I will head on back to my cabin so you two can catch up. Missy, could you please make up Javier and Felicia's room for your brother? It's too late to go back to the city this evening." He tipped his hat, nodded and turned as he started for the door.

I tried to call out his name. My lips mouthed his name but my voice was silent, no words came out.

CHAPTER FOURTEEN

It's been several weeks since I have been back in my town home in Minnesota. I have been back to work a couple of hours a week doing menial tasks as my therapist or my boss won't let me do anything that would cause too much stress right away. Once I was back in my own home and familiar environment, most of my memories have been coming back to me. I have been working with a therapist a couple days a week that is helping me with recollections of my past as far back as my childhood. It is actually nice having J.D. living with me to help me fill a lot of the missing gaps. Everyday more and more of my memories are returning and recollections of events are returning.

I am a different person now than I was before all of this happened. I realized how tightly wound I was. My therapist and I both came to the conclusion that it wasn't just one thing that made me the way I was before the accident but various things, starting with the death of my mother and having big responsibilities placed upon me at such a young age. I felt I had to exceed in my young life to be recognized beyond the twins. They were athletes and very popular. As identical twins they got a lot of attention boosting their egos and self esteem which left J.D. and me in the background feeling as if we were not as important as them.

We each reacted in our own ways; J.D. went one way of rebellion while I felt I had to excel for attention. I felt I had to be strong for J.D. as he struggled through his teen and young adult life. I felt I had to keep everything together to appease dad. Even though he never required me to be 'perfect', I felt I had to try to make everything as perfect as I could so that dad wouldn't have to come home to stress and chaos.

As my days go by here in Minnesota, I often wonder about Bob the Magician, Sunny and Aunt Bev. Even though they were only in my life a few days they had a significant impact on my life, each in their own way. I wondered what they did with Sunny's body. Was she thrown out in a back alley like Bob the Magician wanted only to become one of those 'Jane Doe's' that will never get identified? I wondered if anyone knew her name beside me? Did anyone care enough to ask? Did anyone else know she has family and children back in Chicago?

These things were heavy on my mind and troubled me. I know once I become fully re-acclimated and fully settled in my life here in Minnesota, I am dedicated to making a future trip back to Salt Lake City and look up Bob the Magician and Aunt Bev. I want to personally thank Aunt Bev. I want to thank her for basically saving my life. Without her care, I probably wouldn't have made it through that time.

Someday, I will try and find out what happened to Sunny and try and make sure her girls know that she did truly loved them and missed them. Even though my thoughts drift back to that dark time of living on the streets, more so my thoughts wander back to the ranch as my heart yearns for that time and place.

I miss the spring smells and the fresh morning air. I miss Molly and the puppies. I miss Jason, Sheldon and Miriam and the kids, but mostly, I miss Tommy. I often wonder what he is doing. I often think about our date on horseback and the time he held my hand at the hospital and told me that he would always be there for me. I have avoided contacting him as I know we come from two different worlds and would not be able to have a future together. I often wonder if he misses me as much as I miss him.

It was Saturday morning when my doorbell rang. J.D. just left to go out to his weekly morning Alcoholics Anonymous meeting. Frustrated that J.D. most likely forgot his keys again, I stomped over to the front door to give him yet another scolding for his actions. I whipped the door open and nobody was there. I did a quick glance around and didn't see anyone before looking down. Before me was a large cardboard box sitting on my door step. It had a big red bow on the top. There was a tag on the box that said: "Missing you."

Curious, I slowly took the lid off the box and when I did, I about died when I saw what was inside. It was Oatmeal looking up at me as if he was being punished by being in the box. When he saw me, he perked up and started his little 'yelps' and licking me as I lifted him from the box. He had a little red collar around his neck.

"Oatmeal! Hello my baby. Look how big you have gotten," I squealed in delight. I sat down on the steps and giggled as he licked my face and wagged his tail so hard that I thought he would dislocate his back...much like his mother did the first time I met her. I was in the moment; savoring and enjoying his attention when I realized that someone must have dropped her off. Certainly, UPS or Fed-Ex cannot transport a live puppy across the United States and then drop it off at someone's doorstep without knowing someone was at home.

I looked up and did another 180 degree scan of my surroundings and that is when I saw him; long and lean as if the scene was out of a movie set. Tommy was leaning up against the front fence of my complex with his legs crossed wearing his cowboy hat. Two long black braids were hanging over his shoulders. He was watching me playing with Oatmeal and grinning from ear to ear showing his big dimples.

In shock and surprise, I started to choke up with tears. My stomach did a few flip flops and my heart started to pump faster. With Oatmeal in my hands, I got up and ran towards him. He came towards me as well with arms open wide. We hugged each other tight before Oatmeal started to squirm in between us forcing us to back away from each other. After putting Oatmeal down, I reached up and for the first time, pulled him toward me and french kissed him with as much passion as I could endure as he readily kissed me back. I never wanted that moment to end.

Finally, he pulled away smiling. "I missed you more than Oatmeal missed you," he said.

"I missed you more than Oatmeal too!" I said half smiling and half still crying as we kissed and hugged some more.

This time it was me that finally pulled away. "Come on in, before the neighbors start to talk."

Oatmeal was at our feet and he started to leap and bounce over the grass with his short puppy legs as he followed us into the townhouse. Tommy took my hand as we walked. With Tommy by my side, I felt whole again.

We sat down on the couch and kissed a few more times before the quiet man spoke. "I suppose you wouldn't be interested in coming back to the ranch would you? Jason wanted me to let you know that the fall crew will be coming in soon and they will need someone again for the kitchen and laundry. He said he didn't want to take "no" for an answer but I think it's because he misses your cooking. He apparently has lost ten pounds since you left. He said the food just doesn't taste as good as when you were there."

I smiled at that statement as Jason was a little overweight anyway. "Ah, he could afford to lose another ten pounds," I replied smirking.

"Sheldon's kids miss you too. They miss coming down and seeing you and sneaking cookies and cake from the dessert table. Miriam also said you have to come back as she is tired of being the only adult female out there. Lindsay is always out with her teenage friends so the only female she is left converse with is Molly and Molly although very attentive, isn't a very good conversationalist."

My heart was booming with appreciation and joy. "I don't know...it sounds tempting," I teased.

"I want you back Missy, um Cassie. Every day has been long, and boring. It's so sad when I go into the dining room and you're not there. I miss your face. I miss your smile and your laughter. You gave me something to look forward to twice a day. I don't know how I lived so long without you. I realized that I am in love with you."

The tears started to drip down my face again. The man of little words had a lot to say and it was words that softened my soul to the core as I knew I loved him too.

"Tommy, I want to go back; trust me, I do. You and the ranch were all that I could think of in the last few weeks. There is nothing more I want than to go back there. But..."

As soon as I said the word "but" Tommy's face turned downward towards his lap. I knew by his actions that he was expecting the disappointment which I was about to tell him.

"I cannot afford to work for the summer months only. Where would I go in the winter and what would I do? Besides, I need health insurance and all of that. I am stuck here," I said, realizing the truth and saying the words that I didn't like to hear myself. "I cannot, nor would not, ever expect you to leave the ranch to come here and live the city life. This..." I looked around my townhouse, "this just isn't you."

I felt my stomach start to tense up in knots with the sickened feeling of hopelessness. I knew the bitter truth of the harsh reality of this situation. I felt so sad for Tommy as he was still not looking at me and kept his head down in sadness. Even though I couldn't see his face, I felt his unease. It was as if we never left off with our special connection we had for each other at the ranch. I noticed beads of sweat starting to form on his forehead.

Tommy wiped the sweat from his forehead with the sleeve of his forearm. "I thought you might say something like that, so I came prepared." Tommy apparently wasn't looking down in sadness at my reply but was looking down at his lap. He reached into his pants pocket and pulled out something out of his from pocket.

I was confused and didn't quite understand what he meant from that statement. With his other hand, he gently grabbed my hand and opened it up flat. He placed a lone diamond ring in my opened hand. "Oatmeal and I would love it if you would say 'yes'." At that time, he looked up into my eyes and said, "Please marry me, Missy. I cannot live another day without you."

This time I saw a lone tear rolling down his cheek. "I miss you so much and found myself thinking of you every second and could hardly work. I talked about you all of the time to Jason and Sheldon...I think to a point of nausea. Finally, I think Jason got sick of me always talking about you and said, 'you know you love her so why you are still here? What are you waiting for? Go and get her!' It was not until that moment that I realized how miserable I was without you and how much I love you Missy. I didn't wait another second. I grabbed Oatmeal; jumped in my truck and here I am." He took my hand that had the ring in it; closed my fingers over the ring and kissed my hand ever so softly and said, "I love you so much Missy."

I was in shock. Not in a million years did I even think or expect what had just happened. I couldn't talk. I just sat there wide eyed and dumbfounded as he spewed his love for me.

"I have family health insurance through the ranch and Jason already said we can live in one of the bunk houses on the ranch for as long as we both want or we can get place of our own, and..."

"Stop! Just stop," I put my fingers over his mouth and stop his rambling. "Yes! Yes! I will marry you. I love you too, Tommy!" and flung my arms around him as we sobbed and laughed together in each other's arms.

CHAPTER FIFTEEN

Back to the Ranch

I believe I have become a better person because of my ordeal. I was so hard and focused that I forgot how to stop and smell the roses and how to take the time to love and know people. Living homeless on the street humbled me to appreciate life itself.

I sold my town home and most all of the furnishings contract for deed to J.D. Basically, he is taking over the payments. I traded in my white Lexus for a SUV. I gave most all my career clothes to the local Salvation Army. I realized all of those 'status things' which I thought were so important, were only things. I now live in blue jeans, hoodies and boots or tennis shoes.

I never did get my memory back of the rape and gunshot injury to my head. The last thing I remember is having a drink with a man next to me. I remember his name was a one syllable name like Steve, Mark or Greg but anything after that is missing until the time I woke up next to the dumpster. My new therapist here in Salt Lake City, wants to try and bring out those memories of that time but I have refused. I know I was violently raped, shot and left for dead. Why would I want to live through that ordeal again and again in my mind? So that I can wake up with nightmares night after night? Be afraid to turn every corner in fear of every man I encounter will rape and torture me? I don't want to live my life in hurt, pain and fear. I learned that life is too sacred and precious. I will, however, be a little more street smart for my own safety.

I did give a vague description of the man at the airport bar to Detective Gibson. As far as I know, he may have just been a friendly guy and not the perpetrator at all...however I highly doubt that. Nevertheless, I did agree with my therapist that if some of those memories do start to resurface that I would seek additional counseling to work through it.

One of my first things I did when I got back to the ranch was go back to the Condo in the city. I wanted to know what they did with Sunny and if anyone notified her family. I wanted to see Bob the Magician and thank Aunt Bev for her care. I made Tommy come along with me as I didn't dare go back to that part of town on my own because it was too dangerous. How ironic that at the time I was living there, I didn't think it was such a scary and dangerous place until I got out of there, now I wouldn't step foot in that part of town alone. I also wanted Tommy to come along so I could show him a part of where I came from and lived before coming to the ranch.

When we got to the Condo, the entire building was torn down and only a pile of old bricks remained. There were "KEEP OUT" and "DANGER" signs around the parameter. The owner of the building or the city must have finally bulldozed it down.

As of now, its fall and I am working as the cook again for the fall crew at the ranch, however, the work load remains lighter than this past spring when they had many more temporary helpers.

I make a trip into Salt Lake City once a week with Miriam when she gets supplies. She drops me off at my therapy session and then I take a taxi to the homeless shelter where I volunteer the rest of the day, cooking, serving meals or whatever else I am needed for. When Miriam is done with all of her errands, she picks me up and we go back to the ranch.

I felt pulled to volunteer at the shelter as I wanted to give back what was given to me when I so desperately needed it. Whether it was a simple smile I received from a friendly face or someone who didn't judge me for being homeless, dirty, and hungry or something else, I wanted to give back that which was given to me when I so desperately needed it.

One day, I brought a big sign that I had painted on an old piece of barn wood and hung it on the shelters wall. It was that verse that my Mom insisted I memorize, the verse that has helped me get through some difficult times on more than one occasion: "For I know the plan I have for you, declares the Lord, plans to give you hope and a future. Jeremiah 29:11." I was in hopes the sign would help at least one person. I would be happy that through my Mom and God, we all played a small part and that we made a difference to someone.

Over time, I have asked some of the local homeless people if they ever see Bob the Magician or Aunt Bev, as they tend to all know each other through the various shelters, food banks, etc. Some said that

Bob the Magician was arrested for doing business without a license after several verbal warnings from the city police. What happened to him after his jail time is unknown.

As far as Aunt Bev, none of the homeless people had seen her around any longer and no one knew what became of her, but hopefully she is in a safe place and happy. I will never know what happened to Sunny but someday, I plan on finding her family in Chicago. With a last name of Brettendorf I think it wouldn't be too difficult to find them. Waiting another month or two is not going to change any current status or further outcome. For right now, I have enough on my plate with working at the ranch, counseling, volunteering and planning our wedding this winter. Tommy and I are already talking about having little Tommy's. I have already agreed with Tommy's traditions and to give our children native names and he has agreed to not name our children after any cereals.

I realized after all I have been through, life is good and wonderful and I truly have found my way home.

CPSIA information can be obtained
at www.ICGtesting.com
Printed in the USA
FFOW02n1514080716
25659FF

9 781681 111230